Last Night at Darby's

A Novel by

M a r i a   M c K e o n

Fulton Books, Inc.
Meadville, PA

Published by Fulton Books 2021

ISBN 978-1-64952-592-5 (paperback)
ISBN 978-1-64952-593-2 (digital)

Printed in the United States of America

To Ria and Steph, the greatest loves of my life.

To Lisa, Lori, Mollie, and Traci, who taught me how very much women need one another.

CONTENTS

November 10, 2010

A black Buick Rainier SUV pulls into the driveway, the driver thinking how much she hates the car she is driving. It is too heavy, just like her life. She sighs as she pulls next to her husband's also-black Mercedes. She pulls the key out of the ignition, closes the sunroof, and sighs to herself, "Vacation over. This sucks."

She leans to her right, hits the garage door opener, and peers into the vacuum of retired sports equipment, bicycles, and other child-rearing essentials. Another announcement to no one comes out of her mouth, "Glad you cleaned up the garage like I asked, Kev."

She pops the hatch to the cargo area and begins to empty the contents. The large tailgate cooler comes first, half a case of champagne on top of it. She wheels the tower of indulgence toward the steps to the kitchen and returns for the next round, beach chair and camp chair hung on appropriate hooks in the garage. She muscles her way through pulling out her luggage, pillow, and blanket for one final trip and heaves the massive suitcase up the steps, opens the door to the kitchen, and is greeted by an enthusiastic smile.

He pounces, nearly knocking her against the closing door. "Hi, handsome, I missed you so much!" There are scratches behind his ears and licks on her cheek as she reprimands her loveable Lab. "Get down, Wilson, I'm home, not going anywhere ever again…until next year."

A text comes across her phone, **on a call**.

She sighs again. A year ago, she would have sent him the middle-finger emoji. Today, she does not bother. She lugs the cooler into the kitchen to unpack it. She is just about finished the task when she hears his descent down the stairs from his home office. A container of her homemade caponata is about to go in the fridge as he speaks, "Hi. Whoa, hold up, do not put that away. Any bread left? How was the trip?"

"There's semolina presliced in a baggie in the Wegman's bag on the table. Trip was good. I don't know if Jen and I would have put this together if we hadn't been under so much pressure from the American Heart Association Campaign. Honestly, I know we raised a ton of money, but this trip was the greatest reward from my perspective."

"How'd you get along with Jen's friends?"

Maggie's mind goes to the late-night walk on the beach with Laci, a woman fifteen years her junior and young mother of three. They bared their souls to each other, no pretense or false impressions, and became instant friends. She thinks about Cassie, a woman she instantly connected to because of their shared sense of humor. She wonders if Emily really is as sweet as she seems and smiles at the memory of her dancing to old-school rap songs as she took her shift in the kitchen. She may be sweet now, but no way was she always.

"They're great. I cannot wait to see them again. I wasn't real crazy about Heather, but she's not my friend, so who cares really. Do you remember my friend Sandy? She complained nonstop. She won't be invited next year."

Kevin smiles. "Next year? That means it was a good trip."

"You know, all your golf trips over the years… I finally get it. I'm sorry if I complained about them."

"Mags, it wasn't if."

She eyes him. "Well, the complaining never kept you from going…three times a year."

Kevin pulls a plate from the cabinet and begins to help himself from half the things she just put away. Maggie thinks this is as good a time as any because he probably has another call within the hour. She hands him a small Pellegrino bottle saying, "Here you go. This was on ice the whole trip back. Listen, Kevin, I did a lot of thinking down there."

He continues to eat, lifts his head to look at her, and then puts down his snack. "I figured because I haven't heard from you since the first night. What's the game plan, Maggie?"

"The only way I'm going to know what I want is if I can get some time and space from you, Kevin. It's too hard for me to see things clearly when we are under one roof, beautiful Sunday dinners with the kids and my dad, cocktail parties at the club, which you love and I fake my way through, arguing the whole way to Lindsey's games, and then acting like everything is okay. It's a life that feels disingenuous to me." She watches him return to his food, and a soft smile comes to her. "It's not been all bad, Kevin. I don't want either of us to be angry or bitter. So I'm asking for time and space."

"More space than me traveling five nights a week?"

"Yeah…because all that does is have you land with laundry and fun in your eyes because it's the weekend and then you're out the door again. It's not what I want."

"What do you want, Maggie?"

"How the hell am I supposed to know that when I haven't been free to think about it? I think we should separate. Maybe after Patrick graduates from East."

"That's seven months away, Maggie. Do you really want to do this until then? It doesn't sound like it."

A tear escapes her eye, causing Kevin to go to her. "Don't cry. It's okay. I'm not surprised. You have not been happy for a long time. And you deserve to be…happy with your life. I don't know how to do this, but I guess the extra months will give us time to figure it out. Can we live in denial until the holidays are over?"

"Hell yes! And, Kevin, I am going to take that job with Chester County Scholars. I need to take a shot at it. It will be good for me." She wiggles out of his embrace, only to return with a hug. "I hate that I'm telling you this, but I will always love you. It's just that the love has changed."

"I know… I'm the one that changed it. You're going to kill it in the new job, Maggie." He walks to the kitchen table and clears his plate, taking it to the sink but not the dishwasher, and she thinks to herself, *Fifty percent there…just like my marriage.*

"Look, I gotta get ready for a call," he says, and he is gone, back up the steps.

Suddenly Wilson is up running between the front dining room window and the kitchen door, tail wagging in rapid swings. Maggie smiles as her handsome curly-headed six-foot-three-inch boy with the brilliant-blue eyes bursts through the door. The leftovers Kevin did not polish off are about to be devoured, but not before she gets a welcome-home hug from her son.

Over the next half hour, she learns the crew coach from Trinity College has connected with Patrick, but his heart is set on Tufts, where he applied Early Decision I. "So, Mom, I'll have my acceptance before Christmas! Oh, and how am I going to tell Kristi Raszer I am not interested in going to winter formal with a girl?"

"Well, if you want to go to Tufts, you had better get cracking on the calculus. As for Kristi, it's your call, bud. Are you comfortable coming out to your friends? More importantly, do you have a reason to? And when can I meet him?"

The book bag over his shoulder, half a hug on the way up to his room, he called down the steps, "You'll be the last to meet anyone I'm interested in. Trust me on that one! Oh, and, Mom, Caroline's coming over for dinner after work."

She smiles as her phone lights up with Lindsey's number and thinks the vacation is indeed over. Only three hundred and sixty-five days until she can do it again.

CHAPTER 1

Maggie, November 2014

Maggie hangs up the phone, sighing at the news from Glenn Marshall, CEO, First Federal Bank. The state budget impasse is in a gridlock tighter than a traffic jam on the Schuylkill Expressway, no movement, no end in sight. She clicks onto the e-statement account balance, showing just enough to make payroll but no money for payables. She reminds herself, *Little victories.*

Ping. **Who has fire starters?**

Ping. **Can't vodka start a fire.**

Ping. **Always does at my house on Saturday nite.**

Ping. **Umm, some of us are still working and ur making us THIRSTY!**

A smile begins to spread across Maggie's lips. This has been going on since one thirty. Her girls group, her sisters in shenanigans, her crew, they are her guiltiest pleasure, and she cannot wait to immerse herself in their friendship on the annual no-worries weekend. She hates to ignore them, but she has work to wrap up if she is going to have a chance at enjoying the next four days. She knows the school buses will begin dropping off children within the next ten minutes, and that should take a little wind out of these gals until all are tucked in bed tonight.

Jake pops into her doorway like Kramer making an entrance on *Seinfeld*. "Maggie, you ready?" Ami trails in behind him.

She looks up from her phone, places it facedown, and walks around her desk to the small conference table. "Yeah, sure, come on in. Is Karen with you?"

"Hi, Maggie, did you want me to print the payables for review?"

"Thanks, but no need, Karen. Let's hope we can address those when I return. Now, Jake, let's look at short-term revenue and Ami..." Maggie begins as she puts on her reading glasses.

Ping.

Ping.

Ping, ping.

Maggie relents, "I just got off the phone with Glenn Marshall, and the news from Harrisburg is not good. Their lobbyist reports a target of late January for a state budget, seven months behind schedule. I know other agencies that are closing their doors November thirtieth. This is disgraceful. Our politicians should be ashamed of themselves...starting with the governor!"

Ping.

Karen asks, "Don't you want to check that?"

Maggie jumps up to silence her phone. "Oops, should have silenced that. It's my friends...they can wait." She glances down at the screen to read the last text and tries not to chuckle.

Besides, we need the vodka for Maggie's Bloody Marys.

Turning to her colleagues, Maggie asks, "What's our mantra?"

They reply in unison, "No layoffs. No reduction in services."

"Right! Jake, call PECO and see if you can get a read on the grant, and, Karen, send out the board invoices for their EOY pledges. I will email them tonight before I leave encouraging them to pay early and help us through this cash crunch. Ami, how are your program supplies holding up?"

Ami brightens, and Maggie wishes she could bottle her enthusiasm for the dark days ahead. "We're good, Maggie! I struck a deal with the Food Bank today. They are donating snacks for our after-school sessions for the month of December. They are bursting at the seams with perishable donations from High Grove Orchards and the Bakers Inn. Apples, cider, and donuts for our kids! Bakers Inn is even donating holiday cookies and cocoa for the last sessions in December."

Maggie's heart warms. "God bless them! That is great, Ami. Do you think any seniors will miss the Thanksgiving application deadline? Make sure they know Ms. Maggie is asking, and I'll be out to see any who miss it on December first."

"We're a little worried about Talia. Can we talk about her before you go?"

"Sure thing, just stay put when we wrap up." Maggie turns her attention back to financial matters. "Karen, we have enough to make payroll on Friday and leave $3,000 in the bank."

"Actually, Maggie, it's $2,875.05."

"Yeah, yeah, I know, forgive me for rounding. My point is, we have two weeks to raise $25,000 for payroll and another $5,000 in payables that will not wait...like the rent. Jake, I need you to spend Thursday and Friday calling our top corporate prospects to line up appointments for us to see them all *before* December first. If the governor won't release the education tax credit money, I want to be the first in a long line of beggars that are going to try to get in to see every CEO in the county."

Jake gulps. "I don't know, Maggie, that only gives us ten days when you get back...and five of those are the week of Thanksgiving."

"Yup, and I want to see *all of them*. You know what, Jake? Successful people do not really take holidays off...they are always in. And they will respect the fact that I'm not talking off either... They'll see me. I'm not saying you need to forfeit your holiday. In fact, I do not want you to come with me... This is not going to be pretty. I am not above playing the female nonprofit ED in peril to the heroic CEO. Powerful men love to don the Superman cape, Jake...don't forget that."

Karen gives a chuckle and says, "Anything else, boss?"

"Nope." Maggie turns her attention to Ami.

Karen smiles and says, "And you promise me you'll forget about this place while you're away?"

"Sure thing... Now hit the road, you two, so I can strategize with Ami."

Three hours later, Maggie places her laptop, two grant proposals, her major donor contact list, and the vacation house lease in her bag and wearily locks her office door. It's six thirty, and the sun is starting to set. Her mind drifts to Talia, a girl too gifted not to go to college and too moral to leave her sisters behind in an unstable environment. She will be praying over that one.

Her organization serves students from the worst school districts in the county, all wanting the opportunity to live in safe housing, have enough to eat, and go to competent schools. Food security is a major issue. She knows without proper nutrition, learning is compromised. Maggie wants educational equity for these young people. She wants them to get into college and complete their degrees. She knows the organization needs to develop a parent program to create a sustainable impact in these communities. As she walks to her car, she promises to make the program better and increase the programming to include generational degree completion goals each year.

Ping.

Before shifting her car into first, she reads at text from Cassie.

Hey, I'm at the Acme. I'm not cooking right? Just paper products...

Maggie's turn: **Hell NO, your not cooking!**

Maggie sees the misspelled word and swears to herself, *Damn autocorrect, we're raising grammatical morons with this shit.*

Ping.

She's alive! Matriarch, r u packed yet?

Ping. **Screw the packing—just make sure you have the champagne glasses!**

Maggie turns her phone upside down and drives the short distance home to the sounds of nonstop pinging. The No-Worries Weekend is a mere fourteen hours away, and Maggie is certain that NWW 2014 is sure to be another epic adventure.

CHAPTER 2

Cassie

It has been three weeks since the close of corporate tax season, yet Cassie still feels depleted. The drain is obviously been intensified because she knows she has four glorious days of answering to no one ahead of her. She's excited to see the house Maggie has sent photos of in person and kick around a liberal Delaware beach town for a long weekend. The location could not provide a bigger departure from the confines of her rigid accounting firm.

Cassie pulls her computer bag, purse, and bag of groceries out of her minivan. She is thankful Jen lives across the street for so many reasons, but tonight it is wonderfully convenient to drop her supplies in Jen's garage without her kids picking through everything like seagulls on the beach swooping in to steal a sandwich.

Cassie drops her things on the kitchen table with a thud and calls out, "Hey, anyone home?"

She hears the rumble of Jon's feet heading down the stairs and the slower plodding of her father behind him. "Hey, Mom, did you go to the store?" She waits. Nothing from Emma.

"My day was fine, thanks for asking. And yes, there's cereal and popcorn in there. I know you've had dinner, so go easy, buddy." Cassie gives Jon as much of a hug as he will allow now that he is in seventh grade. He never resists, but he does not hug her back like he used to.

Her dad gives her his version of the same hug. "There's my girl. How was your day, honey? You look tired. Kids and I grabbed pizza after Emma's soccer practice."

Cassie pours herself a diet Coke and says, "Thanks, Dad. What would Doug do without his backup man? I know Emma's old enough to hold down the fort until I get in, but I think Jon loves having one of you run interference with his sister."

Her father digs in his pockets as he grabs his jacket to leave. "I have a message for you, Cassie… Now, where did I put that?"

Cassie's mind immediately goes to the predictable request from her ex. "Please tell me Doug didn't ask you to cover for him after school tomorrow."

"No, no, here it is. It's from Emma's coach. Something about an answer you owe him. Emma has a home game next Tuesday. He's thinking about starting her on varsity. You should get back to him, Cassie. You don't want to piss off Coach Turner."

"Yeah, yeah, Dad, I will."

As her father pulls on his jacket, he gives Jon an elbow. "See ya, buddy. Eagles game, one thirty, Sunday. I'll be making my famous sausage and peppers." He gives Cassie a wink. "Have fun on your trip."

"Thanks again, Dad." Cassie knows Dan Turner does not want to talk to her about Emma's soccer. He wants to take her out for dinner. She thinks Dan is too much, like way too much. If only she could get those words out of her mouth when she sees him. She will text him tonight and delay that answer until after the trip. Hell, after the season. Still, he is not exactly repulsive. He is tall and lean and looks great in that well-worn baseball cap, but Emma… Emma makes everything complicated. She would overdramatize this, of that Cassie is sure.

But before she can think about those gray eyes under that cap for too long, she hears Emma's conniving tone, "Since we have Saturday practice, isn't it just easier for Dad if I stay with Jillian Thursday and Friday night?"

"Nice try. Not happening, not no how, not no way. And your dad already gave me a heads-up you were trying for that. He wants to spend time with you, Emma. Give him a chance."

Cassie pulls laundry from the dryer and starts folding. She glances at the clock while Emma grabs an apple and turns her attention to her phone retreating to her room. Nine o'clock, twelve hours and counting. Laundry, lunches, emails, lists for Doug, and she is out the door!

As if on cue, her phone rings, and she instinctively knows it's Doug calling to check in. "Hello."

"You sound tired. I'm sorry I called your dad, but I got the chance to meet Scott for a drink and talk about the project at Aerzen. Everything okay over there?"

"Yeah, my dad is your ace in the hole, Doug. Don't ever go to Vegas without him."

"No kidding. What's Emma trying to pull?"

"Don't give it a second thought. I shut her down. You are up for the whole weekend, so enjoy them. Dad is coming over for the game Sunday. I'll be home by noon on Monday."

"Yeah, I got it. Any new cast members this year, or you heading out with the same mom mafia as usual?"

"Very funny, yes, same crew. Why mess with perfection? I gotta pack. Good night, Doug…and thanks."

CHAPTER 3

Jen

Mike places the last case of liquor by the garage door, stands back, and smirks. Jen catches his amusement as she brings down her suitcase. "What are you smiling about…four days of peace and quiet or all the alcohol?"

"You girls finish this, and I'm driving your asses straight to rehab when you get back. Seriously, have a good time, but be careful and avoid Heather while you are at it."

Jen looks down at her phone to see a text from Maggie. **Just dropped Wilson at doggie day care b there in 5.**

Jen hears honking in the distance and says, "Get outta here, Mike. That's Laci and Emily turning onto our street!"

"You know the sound of their horns?"

"Who else announces their arrival on a Thursday morning in suburbia?"

Mike shrugs. "Good point. I was kinda hoping for a quickie in the laundry room before you go."

Jen smiles and replies, "You're always hoping for a quickie, and that's why I need this weekend!"

Mike dips her and kisses her for show as the brilliant black Tahoe pulls into their driveway, with Laci raising a coffee mug while popping out of the sunroof. "Got me a coffee with a kick to get things going!"

Emily steps out of the driver's side asking, "We interrupting anything? We can circle around the block a few times if you need time for a little something, something."

Laci is climbing out of the sunroof and sliding off the side of the SUV. "Girl, I told you to take care of the 72 last night!"

Mike is hauling a case of champagne to the back of Emily's SUV. "Seventy-two? Is that a new move? I thought I was pretty well-versed."

Cassie is rolling up the driveway with her luggage and a wagon full of paper goods. "Gee, let me guess who's talking about 72?"

Jen and Emily respond in unison. "Don't ask!"

Laci pulls Mike aside for a little one-on-one sex ed, and Mike starts howling with laughter, "Now you tell me! Jen, we gotta talk when you get back!"

Jen snaps back, "Just get the case of champagne into Emily's rig and go to work, Mike!"

Mike hoists the next case, dutifully heading to the trunk. Emily shifts a large white garment bag to the other side when Mike innocently asks, "What's that?"

Emily answers, "Really, Mike? You should know better. You'll have to wait for the drunken Facebook posts."

The silver Audi convertible whips around the corner, top down, Springsteen blaring, and as Maggie belts out "Rosalita, come sit by my fire," the girls start cheering.

Mike knows when it's time to make an exit. He gives his wife a wink, greets Maggie with a smile, and says, "I thought you were the one to keep them in line."

Maggie retorts, "All in due time, my man, all in due time. First, I need to blow off a little steam."

Maggie and Jen stuff remaining bags, supplies, and bedding into the Audi as the last cooler goes into the Tahoe. Directions are handed out. "Jen, get your scarf and fleece 'cause I'm not putting the top up."

Jen asks, "Seat warmers on?"

Maggie quips, "Who's got your back, woman? Of course they are! And a blanket is in the back seat, you wimp."

Fifty minutes into the drive to Rehoboth, Jen and Maggie are deep into the analysis of the strange relationship between Heather and Jen. Professional colleagues and neighbors, Heather has taken keeping up with the Reagans to a new level. Jen frantically phoned Maggie last week to inform her that Heather had rented a house three blocks from them for this very weekend with her own girls group. Maggie's response was "Of course she did, lame-ass wannabe."

Maggie is devilishly planning ways to shut Heather down should she infringe on their activities when suddenly the Tahoe pulls alongside them revealing Laci, Emily, and Cassie donned in neon wigs and singing Barry Manilow tunes.

Jen turns to Maggie, echoing her annual response to the start of the weekend, "I think this one's going to be epic." Maggie nods in agreement.

They are all suffering from an overwhelming need to leave their worries and responsibilities behind. Jen has just wrapped a major project at work rolling out a new product line for her company. Mike has started his own consulting business, which makes Jen nervous about income. They continue to talk about a baby, and Jen feels the pressure of her biological clock on top of the financial concerns. She and Maggie will be sharing a room. She'd love to vent about this over the weekend because she knows Maggie will listen without judgment.

Jen has no idea how Laci manages it all, four kids, husband that works from home, and a single-income household budget. She would lose her mind if she and Mike were in the house together all day long. How is she ever going to have the patience for a baby?

Maggie senses Jen is drifting inward. She brings her out of her thoughts when she asks her to text the other girls to go straight to the Boat House for lunch while they pick up the house keys from the realtor. "Tell them we're five minutes behind them and order me a Ketel cosmo."

Jen replies, "On it…"

Ping. **The Boat House on Ocean?**

Ping. **Damn, that sounds good! I'll tell them to make it two.**

Ping. **Aww, shit! We r starting w/ the big grl drinks!?!?**

Maggie pulls into Island Realty and practically skips to the office entrance. Jen watches Maggie inside the realtor's office, exchanging pleasantries and charming the locals. Maggie's new best friend, Thom, the realtor, comes into the front office bearing the

20

keys, a bottle of champagne, and some paperwork. Maggie gives Jen a thumbs-up from behind Thom's back as she plants a big kiss and hug on him before sashaying out the door.

She pops in the car. "We can get in at one, and late checkout if we want it. Let me stick the house rules in my purse, but here, you keep this someplace safe for further reference."

Jen asks, "Let me guess, nightlife recommendations?"

"Yup! Thom listed the best drag shows and best karaoke bars! I'll find the cover bands later."

CHAPTER 4

Laci

The Boat House turns out to be the perfect seaside restaurant, complete with fishnets on the walls loaded with fake starfish, plastic lobsters, and shells. The women choose to sit at the bar in order to befriend the female bartender and ask for scoop on local bands and entertainment. The chef serves up amazing crab cakes and fresh salads to complement the round of cocktails from the bar to erase the road trip wear and tear.

Laci's alarm goes off, sending wind chimes across the bar, prompting Jen to hand Maggie the check, saying, "Mags, figure out the gratuity while I ask Tinkerbell to silence her phone."

"Screw you, Jen. Those beautiful notes are the sound a unicorn makes when it farts! And FYI, it also means we can get into the house. Let's go, girls!" Maggie quickly organizes the collection of the first tab of the trip, leaving a healthy tip should they decide to come back, knowing it is never too early to start buttering up the bartenders.

Just blocks away, they arrive at their destination in minutes. The beachfront house does not disappoint, with an open vista of the green Atlantic crashing on the fine, sandy beach just beyond the grassy dunes in front of the house. Jen inhales the salt air before grabbing the thermal bag as Emily reaches for the box of engraved flutes. Maggie and Cassie unlock the door on the first floor as Laci yells from the deck, "Get up here! This view is amazing!"

Maggie hears the beautiful explosion of an uncorked bottle of bottle of champagne as she opens the sliding door to the upper deck and a smile lights up her face. Emily hands out flutes, Laci pulls out her phone for the photo op, Jen pours, and Cassie releases a sigh to signify the official letting go of all concerns from home that only this weekend can bring.

As they raise their glasses, Maggie offers, "Here's to the men who would bail us out of jail and the fun that might land us there!"

Two bottles later after numerous trips to and from the cars, refrigerators are stocked, bar set, and luggage deposited in various rooms. The obvious consensus is to hit the deserted autumn beach and unwind. Laci and Emily rush to their room to suit up, and Cassie calls after them, "This is no *Sports Illustrated* cover shoot. Hurry up!" As Jen and Maggie pack the cooler for the beach, a disruption from the master bedroom explodes on the scene. Emily and Laci appear in neon deep-sea-diver costumes complete with caps, goggles, fins, and oversized inner tubes.

As their audience erupts in champagne-induced howls, Emily deadpans, "Well, a girl might want to go diving for pearls this time of year, so you gotta be prepared!"

As Laci imitates a lifeguard-like muscle pose, a loud hissing comes from her inner tube. "At least you won't drown with those great floatation devices," quips Cassie.

"It's all for effect. You know, set the mood, attract some friends we haven't met yet to stop by and say hi," responds Laci.

Maggie adds, "Oh, we'll attract friends, that's for sure."

Jen slides toward her room, and Cassie asks, "Shit, where are you going? Isn't it a little early for you to jump on the prank bandwagon?"

"If you must know, I peed my pants when I heard Laci's inner tube deflate. Give me two minutes to put my yoga pants on…or head down without me."

By the time the cooler has made it to the ground floor, Jen has caught up and is handing out beach chairs from the garage. The troupe lugs supplies over the dune, selecting a spot close to the beach path in full afternoon sun. Champagne and conversation flow easily from local dirt to *Bravo* updates, eventually onto motherhood and married life. Laci turns toward Maggie with a worried glance, knowing that after three years of separation, Maggie is ready to throw in the towel on her marriage to Kevin.

Maggie wrangles herself out of her chair to stretch, turning to take in the beauty of the ocean. Without explanation or announcement, she heads to the water's edge, rolls up her jeans, and wades in. As the sun warms her back, Maggie's thoughts turn to motherhood. She's years ahead of these girls, with a twenty-six-year-old daughter working in social media marketing on the Main Line, a twenty-four-year-old daughter teaching in Baltimore, and a twenty-one-year-old son in his senior year at Tufts. What a triumph May will bring, the last college graduation and the end of the tuition bills.

If only Kevin could have weathered it all with her instead of watching from the sidelines with growing resentment. Listening to her friends over the years has helped her to clearly identify the issues that disconnected them from each other, eroding her marriage. She wonders if these women know how very much they have meant to her throughout this journey. A new chapter awaits her. She's not the least bit tentative or concerned about what might be next.

Jen quietly approaches the water's edge and interrupts her thoughts. "You okay?"

"Of course, just needed to stretch the legs and be able to get my ass off the sand before imbibing any more champagne."

Jen shrewdly eyes her best bud and roommate, "You ought to tell them soon. They'll understand."

"Oh, I know. I just don't want to be a downer…and for the love of God, no pity party! Do you have my back on that?"

"Always, roomie, always. Hey, you didn't make your bed yet… Is that driving you crazy?"

"Well, it wasn't, until…" Maggie turns toward the others and sees a group of men standing by her empty beach chair, trying to figure out her crew. "Well now, looks like we are making new friends. I swear, it's like bees to honey. Let the games begin."

CHAPTER 5

Emily

As Jen and Maggie return to the group, they hear Emily explain, "No reason or significance… It's all just for amusement. Ours or anyone else's, really."

Jesse, one of the younger men, nods in understanding and says, "Listen, we have a weekly Saturday volleyball game a few beaches down from here. We play unless it's snowing, and even then sometimes. Thing is, your team has to have a name and a uniform of sorts. You all would fit right in."

Laci squeals, "Oh my god, you guys love a costume…am I right?"

Danny, a beautiful, slender, blond Adonis in Lilly Pulitzer capris and aqua cashmere sweater, replies, "We live for costumes, sweetie."

"Hi, I'm Jen. This is Maggie. What do you actually play for? Like, is it just bragging rights?"

Jesse responds, "Oh, hell no, winning team gets a free round at Darby's at midnight. Right, Sean?"

All eyes turn to the man with curly chestnut-and-silver hair carelessly escaping from under the rim of his Dogfish baseball hat. His faded T-shirt and shorts denote middle-aged beach bum who gives zero shits. His piercing dark eyes, however, are fixed on Maggie, making her increasingly uncomfortable. Sean replies, "Jesse is correct…but you have to be there at midnight to get your round… not a minute later."

Maggie offers no smile but takes him in from head to toe before looking straight at him with a challenging glare. It is best he understand that she can give as good as she gets in the stare down they have going on. He does not flinch, holding her gaze, so she turns it up by casting a sweet smile at the others in the group.

Emily is making serious mental notes about this guy. Something about him has piqued her curiosity. "Oh, do you work there?"

"I do."

Jen chimes in, "Okay, one of you guys give us the ground rules on this, and we're in."

Emily instructs, "Danny, these two are late to the conversation. Fill them in."

"We prefer to limit this to four teams, so it doesn't take all day… like, who has time for that? Be there at one, and dress to impress. You girls are so in."

Emily heads over to Sean and offers, "You seem to be the ringleader here. What can we bring?"

"No one leads this group. We just tend to hang together during the off-season. I know pretty much everyone around here, been here a long time." Maggie thinks, *No shit, you act like you own the beach.* He continues, "We'll see who shows up Saturday. As for what to bring, bring your A game, ladies. I'd say bring champagne, but it looks like you might be running low."

Jen perks up at that remark. "Two things you don't have to worry about there, Sean. We always bring our A game, and we never run out of champagne."

Sean breaks into a sly smile, turns directly to Maggie, and asks, "Any other questions?"

Emily's eyes widen in response. Did he just challenge The Matriarch, or is she picking up something else?

Maggie turns an intense gaze directly onto Sean and dryly says, "Well, smart-ass, the address might help." And with that, Emily is certain: sparks are flying. Has anyone else noticed?

Cool as can be, Sean hands Maggie a piece of paper and says, "Text me," swigs his beer, tips his hat, and saunters off.

Danny and Laci are now gyrating, humming, and singing the chorus of "Sexual Healing." Maggie turns, picks up her towel and chair, and snaps, "Fuck off!" before heading to the house. No one is quite certain if she is speaking to Laci and Danny or just Sean.

After a few moments, Emily follows her, leaving Jen and Cassie to find out more about Sean and the bar called Darby's from Jesse. As she approaches the house, she sees Maggie checking the temperature in the hot tub and talking to no one in particular. "Hmm, ninety-four degrees. They must have just filled this today, which is not a bad thing. I'm turning it up a bit so it's ready after dinner."

"Hey," Emily says as a means of announcing herself to Maggie.

"Oh, hey, why did you come up?" asks Maggie as she closes the lid to the hot tub.

"Gotta get my apps together. You know those morons are going to come up here crying for food."

"Let me make my bed, and I'll give you a hand." As they reach the top floor, Maggie stops and asks, "Was I too harsh with Laci?"

Emily chuckles then responds, "Is that even possible? You know she loves you unconditionally. She just worries about you. We all do. You work too much, you spend too much time taking care of everyone in your family, and you're in it alone. You've been separated a long time, Maggie. It's okay to flirt back with someone."

"Why worry about me? What's the difference between me and Cassie?"

"Well, for starters, when Cassie leaves the office, she leaves the office. And Doug helps. He's hands-on…as long as she leaves directions. Besides, a little bird told me there's something brewing between her and Emma's coach."

"Whoa…good for her. Well, if that was flirting down on the beach, I'd say it was a pretty awkward attempt on both parts."

"Maybe not. You still scored a phone number." With that Emily winked and headed for the kitchen. "Let's face it, Maggie Burke… you're hot. And speaking of hot, go make your bed while I call JT. God, I love that man. I get heated just hearing him say hello."

Maggie smiles to herself and says, "Got it, chef! See you in the galley in ten."

What was it about those faded vineyard vine shorts and concert T-shirt that made Maggie's pulse quicken? Damn if he didn't look good walking away. She freely admits to herself that she has a thing for a tight ass with a tight ass.

Maybe the clothes have nothing to do with it. Maybe she just appreciates the good-looking, albeit weathered, man with the hard-as-nails exterior. She suspects that weathering might come from lessons learned, smoothing out his character, just like leather when exposed to the elements. Oh well, she probably won't get to test that theory out. After all, they are here for a good time, not a long time.

CHAPTER 6

Hot Tub Confessional

Cassie appears through the sliding deck door as Emily finishes the food prep and Maggie sets the table. She grabs a bottle of water as she eyes the communal feast Emily whipped up in record time. "Nothing like this would ever come out of my kitchen!"

Maggie looks around for Jen and Laci. "You didn't leave those two on the beach in the dark did you, Cassie?"

Bang! "Honey, we're home!" *Pop!* "And we brought provisions... Seven bottles down, but we're still standing." Laci makes the rounds, topping off empty flutes and searching for the portable speaker to fire up the music. "Jen, Spotify me, Momma!"

Jen calls up the steps, "Divas or dudes?" Before anyone can answer, Pink's "Blow Me One Last Kiss" fills every room, spilling out to the deck through the still open slider. Her entrance into the great room is nothing short of theatrical with a hot-pink boa flowing with every move and twirl. She is sporting a white cap embroidered with pink flamingos and "Stop Flocking Around."

Maggie and Emily raise their glasses, scurry to move the oversized ottoman from the center of the great room to open up the dance floor, and lay the food out for grazing between dances. Two hours, three champagne bottles, four bags of chips, and five fits of laughter later, the dance-weary women settle onto the sectional couch to prioritize the weekend ahead.

"How about a little Lionel, Jen," asks Emily. "Maggie, what's the game plan for tomorrow?"

"No real plans other than I'm in charge of lunch and finding a bar with a Friday-night cover band. I mean, we really cannot waste these moves on just us all weekend. Where's my phone? I'll sleuth it out."

"No, no, no technology beyond tunes tonight. It's hot tub time!" responds Cassie.

Jen is up like a shot. "I thought you'd never ask!"

Maggie is the first to head out to the hot tub, delighted to find Emily and Laci's whimsy has illuminated the upper deck with white lights, strung pink flamingoes, and two inflated palm trees. She turns on the jets, tosses her towel over the railing, and slips into the deliciously hot water. Leaning back, head on the edge of the tub, Maggie's mind drifts to Kevin and her children. She feels certain the girls support her decision, but she knows her son worries. Patrick has successfully navigated his way through college in order to graduate on time. He feels ready to leave the protective-bubble Tufts, but freaks out about the uncertainty of postbaccalaureate life. Add his parents' divorce, his final crew season, a serious romance, and nagging sisters into the mix, and Maggie shudders at the emotional roller coaster. His mind must be swirling with greater turmoil than the water bubbling up around her.

Splash! "Hey, move over. No bogarting the bench seat," insists Cassie. "Besides, there are three more behind me bearing gifts."

Maggie reluctantly skootches over as the slider opens to reveal Jen and Emily bringing flamingo hats for all. "Each of us have our own saying," Jen proudly declares. "Cassie, 'I don't give a flock' is all you. Emily, you've got 'Calm the flock down.' For Maggie, 'Stand by your flock.' And may I have a drum roll please…behold, the lovely Laci Holbrecht sporting 'I don't give two flying flocks.'" Laci appears with a cap that has flamingo wings flapping, flamingo head bobbing from the top, a neon-pink bikini, and tray of pink panty-dropper Jell-O shots.

"Cheers time, girls, down the hatch!"

Jack Johnson, Jimmy Buffet, and Kenny Chesney are dominating the playlist. Laci passes the Jell-O shots once again and asks, "Anyone need a little more truth serum? You know what's coming next ladies, right?"

In unison, they respond, "What is, something that has changed about you since last year?"

"I'll go first," claims Laci. "How about my hair?"

Cassie rolls her eyes. "Oh, puhleeze, that changes every month!"

"Okay, okay…hmm. I changed my church…and now I actually go!" Laci slips underwater to emerge between Cassie and Maggie, turns to Cassie, and says, "Your turn."

"I didn't fire anyone this year… Does that count?"

Laci reaches for the shots. "Nope! Since we both gave lame answers…shot, shot, shot!"

Cassie giggles, takes her shot, and blurts out, "All right, all right, I met Dan Turner for coffee three weeks ago."

"Ohhhh," the peanut gallery responds.

Jen quickly jumps in, "Was it to talk about Emma's sick bicycle kick?"

"Well, I thought it was team related…"

"Oh yeah, the old 'let me have coffee with my daughter's hot soccer coach.' Totally normal. 'Fess up, woman," teases Laci.

"There's nothing to tell. One dark roast black for him, a caramel macchiato for me, awkward start, a few laughs in between, and that's it. Nothing more to see here."

"Whoa, cowgirl, not so fast there," says Emily. "You've had no other contact, no other communication?"

"I didn't say that. He wants to go out to dinner, but my answer is one word: Emma. It's so not worth it."

Emily strategizes, "Unless she moves up to varsity…then Mr. Turner isn't her coach anymore. Does she have him for math?"

"Uh, no. Turner teaches honors and AP classes…not Emma's strong suit."

"Well, it's all settled. Emma needs to move up to varsity, because she's freakin' awesome. And if she has to sit the bench for the rest of the season, well, it's the least she can do for her mother."

Laci dips under water again, expertly balancing the shot tray above the bubbles. She pops up in front of Emily, proclaiming, "You know the rules, challenge the truth teller and you're next."

"Bring it, sister, 'cause I'm ready." Emily slurps her shot and confidently proclaims, "I quit the PTA last night." High fives all around.

"Pray tell why, my dear," asks Laci.

"Well, after three years as incoming president, president, and outgoing president, I just hit the wall. That, and that bitch Heather Lewis kept saying 'Must we repeat the mistakes of the past each year.' So I just said flock it!"

After peals of laughter die down, Jen chimes in, "Heather Lewis can't hold a candle to you, Em. And that wench couldn't come up with an original idea if her life depended on it. She imitated all of my work when we were at Liberty together."

Cassie adds, "And now she's imitating Jen's life. Like, why of all the neighborhoods in our school district did she have to move into ours? And then paint her house just like Jen's, ask her for her landscaper, ask her about a handyman, and so on… Ugh, creep!"

"Tell me about it, she told me the other day that she wants Joel to work from home, just like Mike. What street are she, Angie, and their crew staying on?"

Laci pirouettes in Jen's direction. "Eighth… Nice try, but no deflecting. Join me and let's have it, Jen."

Jen and Laci raise their shot cups. Jen dramatically tosses hers back and blurts out, "I've learned to say maybe."

Laci unsteadily leans in, "Maybe what?"

"Maybe we should have a baby," Jen murmurs.

"What? That's so exciting! Are you serious?"

"Easy, Lace… I think the operative word here is *maybe*," cautions Maggie.

"Yeah…exactly. Do you know the term for women my age who are with child?" asks Jen. "It's called a geriatric pregnancy. I mean, what the hell is that? If that doesn't say this is not a good idea, what does? But Mike would be a great dad…and he is just so happy when we talk about it."

Maggie adds, "Don't cut yourself short. You'd be a great mother... Look at how seriously you're thinking about this. Just know what you and Mike have will never change. That man loves you. You alone are enough for him, if that's what you decide."

A champagne tear escapes Jen's eye. Laci faces Maggie. "Oh, wise one...what will the serum release from you?"

"No shot. That shit will kill you. Brace yourselves, girls... I'm divorced."

Silence.

Finally, Laci responds, "Wait...what?"

"Yup, signed, sealed, and delivered to the courthouse on Monday," explains Maggie.

"Oh my god, I have to text Danny..." Laci attempts to climb out of the hot tub, but Maggie strong-arms her.

"Danny who?"

"Capri pants Danny, my new BFF!"

"And why would you feel the need to tell him this? And when the hell did you have time to get his number?"

"Because he said Sean was totally into you...and you got Sean's digits way before I got Danny's. I was just following your example, because you're my hero. Plus, Danny wants us to come to the Parrot to see his drag show Sunday night."

"Well...no, he's not, you're ridiculous, and I can't wait for Sunday!"

The others respond in unison, "Yes, he is, yes, she is, and yeah, we're going!"

Laci gives Maggie a wet hug, winks, and asks, "So have you texted him?"

"Of course not. Cocky son of a bitch, 'Text me.' Yeah, I'll get right on it."

"Aww, come on!" Laci pleads.

"I'm not even sure where I put his number when I came in... Champagne brain will do that, you know."

"Oh, no worries, roomie. I saw it under your phone on the nightstand," offers Jen.

"Busted!" cries Laci.

Maggie just smiles. How could she possibly get mad at this crew? In an attempt to redirect the conversation without being completely obvious, Maggie offers, "So this volleyball game…are we all in?"

"Oh, hell yeah we are," exclaims Jen. "We need to bring it, ladies!"

"Considering Cassie started four years at Penn State, you played every summer at the Jersey Shore, and the rest of us are just a tad competitive…bringing it should be no problem," offers Maggie.

Jen tries to clarify, but the shots are kicking in, "Noooo. The theme, we need a theme!"

Maggie stands to make her way to the edge of the tub, takes off her cap, waves it at Jen, and says, "I think we've got one: birds of a feather flock together. I'm hitting the shower. See you inside. Please don't let Laci drown before I come back."

"Seriously, Mags… I'm buoyant as a buoy."

Maggie grabs a bottle of water and heads toward her room to collect towel and pajamas. She quickly sneaks into each of the girls' rooms to leave a little gift on their pillows, a delicate sea glass necklace for each woman with a note explaining that each necklace is as individual and beautiful as they are. She walks toward the hall bathroom, with the sound of laughter and Bob Marley in the background, tosses her towel by the sink, and steps into the shower.

Emily is leaning over the hot tub, waiting for Maggie to shut the bathroom door, and exclaims, "Now!" She hops out to wrap up in a towel as Laci scurries past her toward Maggie and Jen's room, sliding on the hardwood floor of the hallway like Tom Cruise in *Risky Business*. Once in the room, Laci tiptoes toward the nightstand.

"Now you're quiet? What are you doing?" asks Emily. "Just grab the phone and his number. Tuck the charger cord behind the nightstand, and let's go before we get caught."

"I need the passcode," laments Laci.

"Give it to me! We'll figure that out later. I mean seriously, it's either her birthday, birth year, or house number."

Emily should feel guilty but doesn't. She won't let this get out of hand, and should Sean never text Maggie back, no harm done. She grabs the phone from Laci, opens the door to her bedroom, and tucks it under her pillow for later, wondering, *How late is too late to text a grown-ass man that works in a bar?* Then she smiles to herself. He's going text back, she's sure of it.

Emily places the small brown box tied with kitchen twine on her nightstand, knowing this is Maggie's work. Organic wrapping around a treasure, thoughtful always, in spite of the million things she has to take care of. She wonders who takes care of Maggie, and in that instant, she pulls out Maggie's phone, punches in 1963, and unlocks it. *Ha, piece of cake*, she thinks. She enters Sean as a contact and types, "Address???" knowing her friend would offer little else by way of encouragement. She quickly silences the phone and tucks it back under her pillow before joining the others.

CHAPTER 7

Hungover As

Maggie has tried to fall back to sleep long enough. She knows her internal clock well. It's time to get up. Quietly feeling around in the dark for a pair of pants, she moves slowly being careful not to stub her toe or wake Jen. Why she would bother is beyond her, considering the raucous shenanigans that wound down just hours ago. She outsmarted them as they tiptoed toward her bed with loud stage whispers and the squeaky noise from the giant flamingo they were attempting to plant in her bed. When she could feel their presence near her, she shot up with a loud, "Boo!" which scared the daylights out of their drunk asses.

Maggie's foot hits her duffel bag. Score! She reaches down, feels yoga pants. Double score! Digging further, she grabs something super soft, some underwear, and a sports bra. Good enough.

Emerging from her room with stealth-like precision, she flips on a table lamp and eyes the bar. Yikes! The kitchen appears to be somewhat tidy, but no coffee maker out. After a quick scan for her phone, she decides it can wait until after her walk. She heads to the downstairs bathroom and smiles at her blind wardrobe picks. Black Athletica ankle pants, her sea-green cashmere wrap, a faded sports bra, and equally pathetic underwear. It could be worse. At least the gray Henley she slept in will add a layer by the ocean. Honestly, did she pack in the dark?

A quick brush of her now-out-of-control beach waves, and she is out the door. She walks toward the Audi to find her car door unlocked. Score again! She rummages through the glove compartment for Chapstick and change to find her emergency twenty dollars and promptly shoves both in the inside flap pocket of her pants.

The sky is brightening, although she can't see the sun from behind the grassy dune. Wondering what time it is and cursing herself for misplacing her phone, she heads for the beach path. The sight at the end of the path does not disappoint. Maggie pauses to take in the brilliant-white caps against the nearly-navy-blue water in the early morning hours. The sun's rays are peaking through the cumulus clouds with enough golden illumination to light up the horizon.

As Maggie reaches the water's edge, she kicks off her flip-flops and rejoices in feeling the cold sand as saltwater laps her ankles. Facing the Atlantic, breathing in the crisp air, she pulls her wrap fully around her and decides to head north, thinking the sun will be high enough to warm her face for the walk back.

Numerous blocks into her walk, Maggie sees other early risers heading down for a stroll or jog. An elderly man approaches and gives her nod. "What a morning!" Maggie smiles, and he stops cold. She stops as well. "I'm sorry, did I startle you?"

"No, you just look like someone I knew, especially in that wrap," answers the man.

"Well, I hope she was lovely and kind, but I suspect she was a little Irish, so that's a total crap shoot."

The man chuckles and reaches out to shake Maggie's hand. "My name's Jim, and yes, she was more than a little Irish. I left her there at the end of World War II, but I've never forgotten her curls, her round eyes."

"I'm Maggie. Trust me, you probably saved yourself a lot of trouble. Women like me are a volatile lot. We lead with passion instead of reason and are slow to change our ways. World War II vet, and you are up and walking the beach? You might have given her a run for her money."

Jim offers her a wide smile and a wink before saying, "I hope you've met someone to give you a run for your money, Ms. Maggie."

Before Maggie starts to walk away, she counters with "Not yet, Jim, not yet."

Maggie puts her head down, flattered by the compliment Jim gave her saying she reminded him of a girl from over fifty years ago. *Jim's vision is obviously compromised*, muses Maggie, but God bless him, he made her day.

Several blocks later, her mind has drifted to the responsibilities of her job. She has decided to take Talia for a personal interview at Swarthmore College in order to give her every advantage should she choose to apply early decision. The school will challenge her academically and provide every opportunity for personal growth. The campus is just far enough so that she will have to board and close enough that she can get home if needed. Deep into mentally laying out the details of her plan for Talia, Maggie notices a shadowed silhouette angling toward her. She lifts her head to see how far she has walked and is stunned to find a somewhat familiar face. Damn it!

"Well, hello there. You're up kind of early for someone on vacation." Sean's greeting has her temporarily tongue-tied. What is wrong with her? Maggie shades her eyes with her hand and takes in Sean's walking companion, a one-hundred-pound-plus Rottweiler.

She takes the opportunity to change her focus from the nicely fitting Elvis Costello concert T-shirt, jeans, and rainbows to, isn't this is interesting, Sean's female rottie. She crouches down a bit and greets the dog, "Hello, gorgeous. Oh, and you too, Sean. Is she friendly with strangers?"

"Depends," Sean replies.

Damn it, he's so intense with his eyes. Oh shit, thinks Maggie, *no makeup*. Instead, she resumes eye contact with the dog and counters, "I won't overwhelm her. What's her name?" The dog is starting to wag her tail, relaxing her ears as her jaw transforms into a canine smile.

"Rosalita DeMarco, affectionately known as Rosie," offers Sean. "Go for it. You've got her approval." Maggie muses, *A Springsteen fan, interesting*.

Maggie begins by offering the back of her hand to Rosie, allowing her to sniff and feel secure. She crouches down and gently pats Rosie's head, working her way toward the back of her ears and offering a full cranial massage. Rosie steps into Maggie's personal space, encouraging a vigorous back and eventual hip rub.

Sean laughs while chastising her, "Rosie, mind your manners."

"She's obviously starved for affection, poor girl. Seriously, she's lovely. I always thought this breed got a bum rap."

"Oh, I wouldn't mess with her, but yes, she's a lover when she trusts. So I gather you are a dog person?"

"Guilty. I have a handsome black lab mix named Wilson waiting for me at home. I would show Rosie his picture, but he'd only break her heart. That, and I can't find my damn phone."

"It happens. I could call it for you later, if it helps. FYI, you're pretty far from your house. What time did you hit the beach?

"I don't know... No phone, remember?" smiles Maggie. "Sunrise, actually. And how are you going to call me without my number?"

"How much champagne *did* you drink last night?" teases Sean.

"Oh, I shut it down before midnight, but it's safe to say we put a dent in the first case. Wait, why do you ask?"

"You really don't remember texting me?"

The confusion on Maggie's face changes to dread. "Are you playing with me, Sean? Because I am not amused."

"Someone's in trouble, but it shouldn't be me." Sean starts to pull his phone from his jeans as he juggles Rosie's leash and pauses. "The proof is in here, but it could take a while for you to sift through your messages to me. I know a great place for coffee right off this beach path. Can I buy you a cup?"

Maggie hates to admit it, but she is jonesing for a cup. She pulls her wrap a little tighter around herself, widens her eyes, and casts them toward Sean as she replies, "If there's coffee and the root of this story wherever we're headed, I'm in."

"Good Lord, woman, how much trouble has that look gotten you into? Let's go before I change my mind."

Maggie peppers the conversation with small talk, what part of the island Maggie has walked to, are the beaches free, is there a wetlands protection organization here, and before she realizes it, Rosie is heading up the steps of a beautifully restored 1920s beach bungalow a block and a half off the beach. "I'll wait here while you let her in."

"You don't have to. The best coffee in town is inside. Come on, trust me."

Oh shit, what am I doing? thinks Maggie. No phone, no idea what street she's on or what this guy is all about. Oh, what the hell, coffee sounds great, and she can't get answers to her questions without going in. As Sean DeMarco opens the screen door, Maggie takes in a full view of him in those Seven jeans and flies up the steps like she hasn't a care in the world, hoping he doesn't sense her anxiety.

"Powder room is on the right, just past the living room. Coffee will be ready in a few. Come on, Rosie, you deserve a treat for being such a good girl." With that, Sean moves to the kitchen. Maggie is dying to take in the living room but makes a beeline for the powder room instead. One look in the mirror, and Maggie is grateful for rosy cheeks and curly hair. *Well, a good look at me now and that should take the rose off the bloom,* she thinks. *Let's get to the bottom of this.*

She offers, "Can I help?"

"Nope, just gave Rosie a bone to keep her from pestering you. Let's head out to the porch. I'm right behind you." *Darn it,* thinks Maggie, *no time for sleuthing!* As she walks to the screen door, a photo of two men attracts her attention. The younger man is undoubtedly Sean's brother, and the other must be his partner. There's love there. It transcends the photograph and warms her heart. She briefly thinks of Patrick before hearing Sean's steps leaving the kitchen.

"The least I can do is hold the door." He smiles. And as Sean approaches, she adds, "French press? Okay, you weren't kidding about the coffee. Thank you!"

As Maggie lifts the clay mug to her lips, Sean pours his own mug and says, "Before we go any further, there's one request, actually a condition."

"Go on," Maggie says, fully engrossed in the aroma and warmth of her coffee.

"I would like you to answer three harmless questions."

"Harmless? I'll be the judge of that. Proceed."

Sean takes his first sip, savoring over it for just a moment. "All right, number 1, what's your name?"

"Maggie."

"Full name, please."

"Okay, but you asked for it. Maggie Kennedy O'Rourke Burke. And just in case you are wondering, I was born on November 22, 1963. My dad insisted on Kennedy given the circumstances."

"A respectable request. Number 2, and I need you to be honest because I'm probably going to google you, are you married?"

"I'm not. Divorced. Offering no other details except to say there's nothing bitter about it."

"Enlightened, nice. Mountains or beach?"

"Love a lake but hate the Poconos. Beach!"

"All very insightful, thank you for indulging me. I truly hate to interrupt what has been a very nice morning, but we'd better get to the matter at hand." Sean digs his phone out of his pocket, punches in his password, and scrolls to the top of her text trail. He places his phone on the coffee tray and slides it in her direction.

Maggie suddenly doesn't want to see this in front of him. "Wait, how bad is it?"

"It's not that bad, just lengthy… I was kind of flattered at first honestly but thought you were either overserved or sabotaged. Seeing you today, I'm convinced it's the latter."

"Thanks for that. You know what? I will just delete it all when I get back to the house."

"As long as you don't delete my number, I'm cool with that."

"Don't give me reason to."

"Noted." Sean takes his phone back as Maggie sees an incoming call from Becca. *Also noted*, she thinks. Sean picks up. "Hey, what's up?" Pause. "Don't worry, I'll be in within the hour."

Maggie allows herself a mental sigh, *Whew, it is just work.* Again, what is she doing? Sean interrupts her thoughts, "How about I give you a ride home? It's almost ten, and someone is bound to be worried about you."

"I'd appreciate it. And, Sean…" She pauses to catch his gaze full on. "Thank you for not embarrassing me."

"Embarrass you? Maggie Kennedy O'Rourke Burke, I'm trying to impress you." And there it is, the dark, intense, soul-searching gaze that leaves Maggie completely depleted of resolve. "Let's go. Jeep or Harley?"

"Jeep…this time." And with that, she swears she sees Sean DeMarco's weathered persona soften just a bit.

The Jeep is a vintage 1980, something Wrangler, meticulously maintained. Sean grabs a towel from the behind the passenger seat to wipe it off, explaining, "Sorry, but you'll be sitting in Rosie's seat. This should keep some of the dog hair off you." He closes her in and slides in the driver's seat.

"No problem. I mentioned I have a Lab, right?" Maggie takes in the utilitarian chrome dashboard, floorboard stick shift, and functional steering wheel before noticing the wooden beaded necklace with a St. Christopher's medal pinned to the clasp. "How old is this Jeep? Clearly made before they mainstreamed it. It has that military vibe despite the red."

"It's an '85. Came with the house and I can't part with it, so I keep throwing money into it. I actually have to play cassettes if I want music."

"What's a cassette?"

Sean shoots her a look of exasperation, and Maggie bursts out laughing. "Easy, Sean, I had cassettes, and even worse…" Together they say, "8-tracks." Maggie leans her head back and closes her eyes to let the wind run through her hair. The sun is warming up the island. She's feeling a sunny and seventy-degree day ahead.

Sean makes a mental note that this is the first woman that did not ask him to put the roof on with temperatures hovering at sixty degrees. He crosses over Rehoboth Avenue to take an easy left onto Norfolk and slows the Jeep to neutral. "You ready for a million questions?"

"I had thought about asking you to drop me off a block ago, but no. They made their beds, now they're going to have to lie in them. Pull right up in front of the house, yellow house on the right, all the way down on the beach block."

"Happy to be of service, ma'am…but first." Sean reaches across Maggie, opens the glove compartment, and pulls out "Tape no. 5," inserts it, and turns the dial so that the Stones' "Gimme Shelter" is just loud enough to make an entrance. She sends him an evil but very approving smile. He waits for the lyrics and watches her begin to dance in her seat before saying, "Now you're ready."

He idles next to the Audi, gives the convertible the once-over, and pronounces, "Ms. Burke, you're holding out on me."

"You have no idea, Sean." Maggie smiles. "Thanks for a great Friday morning." She reaches for the door before things get more awkward.

"Maggie, wait." Sean pulls up the emergency break, shuts down the Jeep, pops out, and walks over to get her door. "I'm sure you girls have your own plans tonight, but you're welcome at Darby's anytime."

"Yeah, thanks, maybe. We kind of fly by the seat of our pants this weekend." Maggie's mind announces to her that she is officially way past awkward.

"How about this, I text you this time." Sean takes her hand as she gets out of the Jeep and walks her to the back door without letting it go. Maggie isn't certain, but she thinks she may be breaking out in a sweat. As if on cue, the giant flamingo is precariously lowered from the top deck with a sign reading, "Where have you been?"

Sean laughs, "Good luck," gives her a kiss on the cheek, and is off down the road.

Maggie braces herself for the inquisition as she climbs the stairs, flamingo in tow. She sees Emily and Jen on the deck, Cassie pouring a cup of coffee. "Want one?"

"Had some" is all she will offer.

She shoves the flamingo onto the deck. "Funny, hilarious in fact."

"Where have you been, young lady?" asks Jen. "Do we know that boy's parents?"

Maggie glares. "Where is Laci? I'm only saying this once."

Emily looks to Jen and back to Maggie as Cassie hands Maggie a mug of coffee anyway. "Umm, Laci is kind of indisposed at the moment."

"Well, get her up, 'cause I'm pissed."

Laci pokes her head out of the slider and moans as she faces the bright sun. "Don't get stirred up, buttercup. What's wrong? What did I miss?"

"Maggie has been MIA...like, for hours," blurts Jen. "But not to worry, she found her way home thanks to tall, dark, and edgy."

"What?"

Maggie hands Laci the coffee. "Here, you need this more than I do."

"Thanks, Mags...but seriously, what did I miss?"

Maggie waits for her to take a sip. "You know what I've missed, Laci? Jen? Em? Cassie?"

Cassie scans the others. "Okay, I'll bite. What have you missed?"

"My goddamn phone, that's what!"

"Oh, I've got it, Mags." Emily moves to retrieve it, but Laci stops her.

"Umm, no you don't, Em." Laci reaches into her tank top and pulls the phone out of her bra.

"Beautiful, let me have it," demands Maggie.

"Wait!" yells Jen. "I don't think you're ready for this."

Maggie aggressively grabs the phone and accesses her text messages. There he is, top of the list above Patrick's text from yesterday. She opens it and sees a strand of blue bubble messages, the number of which appalls her. She's swiping furiously until she gets to the top, 10:05 blue bubble "**Address???**" followed by a gray bubble thirty minutes later "**Prospect St beach...glad u can make it.**" The next blue bubble is at 12:42, "**I bet u r.**" Maggie closes the text to prevent herself from reading the rest. She swipes the conversation and announces, "In the interest of our friendship, we will never discuss this again."

"We're sorry, Maggie," offers Jen.

"I said NEVER."

"Okay, but where were you this morning?" asks Cassie.

"I took a walk on the beach. Met a sweet eighty-five-year-old man named Jim, a hot bitch named Rosie, and ran into Sean. I had walked pretty far, and he offered me a lift back here. End of story."

"Sean brought you home?" Laci reaches back into her tank top and pulls out her phone to text Danny an update, and Cassie breaks the tension by saying, "What the hell, Laci, do you have the whole Verizon store in there?"

As the five dissolve into a fit of laughter, Laci mutters, "Shit. I'm hungover as fuck, I can barely text." Maggie rolls her eyes, Emily smirks, Jen throws her hands up, and Cassie gently reaches over and turns the phone right side up.

Maggie offers, "Bloodys, anyone?"

CHAPTER 8

Hell Yeah I'm Scared

The Bloody Marys revive the troops, encouraging a "let's get our shit together" spirit among all. Conversation turns to tomorrow's volleyball game, their uniforms, and their team name. After hashing out numerous flamingo alliterations and under Jen's marketing prowess, they settle on the Flock of Femme Fatales.

Maggie picks up her phone, and Laci immediately inquires, "Checking for anything in particular there, Mags?"

"Yup, checking to see if I should start lunch. And I should, so you all figure out a team uniform to go with our hats, and we'll eat in thirty."

Maggie heads to her domain, the kitchen. After rummaging through cabinets for a stock pot, she carefully empties the container of her homemade butternut squash and green apple bisque, setting the burner to medium low, lid on. Digging through her grocery bags, she grabs the loaf of marathon bread, honey mustard, walnuts, and raspberry preserves. Heading to the fridge next, she pulls the wheel of double cream brie, shaved Virginia Ham, butter, and fresh green apple from their buried places on the shelves.

Sounds of Motown fills the house, and Maggie dances as she cooks. Laci comes in to help and immediately joins in the dance moves to the Four Tops as she sets the table. Job completed, she hugs Maggie from behind saying, "You know I love you and never wanted to piss you off." Maggie shakes her head, smiling but saying nothing.

Maggie slips a cookie tray of chopped walnuts into the preheated oven, asking Laci to put down wineglasses as she builds the sandwiches. Pulling deep ice cream bowls from the cabinet closest to the table, she fills the sink with hot water and drops them in. Maggie pulls toasted walnuts from the oven, the green apple is diced, and the sandwiches are placed on a piece of parchment paper on the cookie sheet and inserted into the oven. Four minutes later, sandwiches are flipped, tray turned, and bisque stirred.

Laci comments, "I swear, Mags, it's like watching a ballet when you're in the kitchen. Your kids are grown. Can't you just move in with me and cook at my house?"

"Anytime, Laci, anytime. I have some sauvignon blanc in the cooler outside. Will you bring two bottles in? And tell the girls lunch is ready."

The girls gather around the table with appreciation and anticipation in their eyes. Maggie works the crowd as she opens the wine. "Please sit down. Today we are serving an autumn butternut squash with toasted walnuts and crisp apples along with an organic harvest salad, grilled brie, raspberry and ham sandwich. Vegetarian options are on the edge of the platter."

Jen offers, "Have we ever told you how happy we are that you grew up in your dad's restaurant?"

Emily pours the wine. Cassie claims the dish duty as Maggie takes off her apron, taking her seat at the head of the table. Laci takes a picture of her soup and salad and posts it on Facebook with the caption, "Maggie in the house... YUM!"

"Take that, Heather!" Jen mugs for a photo dramatically dunking her sandwich into her soup bowl. Snap, post.

"Aww, Danny wants to come for lunch," Laci reports.

Jen immediately shuts that down, "Aww, hell no, we have serious stuff to take care of. Tell him we're here for two more days, not to worry." Jen begins laying out her ideas for a uniform, which includes tulle, boas, ribbon, and sequins or glitter. After a quick search, a Walmart is found up island, and the unshowered members of the group, Maggie and Laci, clean up their acts as the others clean up from lunch.

As Maggie towel dries her hair, her phone rings. It's Caroline, her oldest. "Hi, sweetie, what's up?"

"Hi, Mom, how's the trip?"

"Weather is gorgeous, sunny, and seventy-five yesterday and a duplicate today."

"That's great, I'm glad. Listen, Mom, don't be mad…but Dad asked me to come take over with Wilson."

"What? Why?"

"One of his clients called him. He's on the way to Dallas to watch the game from the AT&T box on Sunday."

"I'm sorry, honey, does this screw with your weekend?"

"Not at all, but as long as I have you on the phone, don't be mad if we hit up your wine tonight. Jack and I might have a few friends over."

"That's fine, but stay away from the French stuff, okay? And how's my boy?"

"Wilson is a trip, Mom. He doesn't skip a beat as long as one of us is with him. Go have fun."

"Thanks, love." Maggie disconnects thinking that Kevin Burke is also a trip. Oh well, no longer her problem. *Have fun, buddy, life is short.* No sooner does she complete that thought when…

Ping.

You r holding out on me. Danny just showed me your lunch photo!

Many talents my friend…many talents.

I'd like 3 more questions.

Choose carefully…heading out w grls, talk later?

100%.

Maggie thinks to herself, *Life is short indeed.*

Jen walks into their room, surprised that Maggie isn't ready. "The natives are getting restless. You about ready?"

"Sorry, Caroline checking in. Mascara, lip gloss, and I'll be good to go. Two minutes, I promise."

Fifteen minutes later, and the women pile out of the Tahoe, game faces on to brace the Saturday crowd found at any Walmart in America. Laci and Em head for the Halloween sales racks, Cassie and Jen head to find tulle, and Maggie heads to makeup. After scoring raspberry lipstick, blush, pink glitter eye shadow, and black eyeliner, she searches the aisles for her friends.

Jen and Cassie appear in the center aisle carrying bolts of pink and black tulle along with five spools of wide pink satin ribbon. Emily and Laci pop out of aisle 7 donning powder-pink pageboy wigs. "There are only two left, but I think we need them," claims Emily.

"They are all yours," remarks Maggie.

Emily holds up a bag of pink extensions. "Not so fast there, madam. It's all in the name of glory. Do it for team spirit."

Maggie offers her basket of cheap makeup for review, and they all smile in anticipation. As if a beacon in the night, a large jar of pink glitter in a carousel by the registers call out to them. As Jen goes to grab it, Emily yells, "No way! I'll never get that out of my car."

"What if we Uber there and home and glitter up on the beach path?"

"Done deal."

Forty-one dollars and change later, their uniforms are all but set. As they pull out of the parking lot, Heather's minivan pulls in. Jen and Cassie duck in the back seat, and Maggie starts laughing. "It's a small town, girls. It's gonna happen."

"Let's hit the boardwalk while we're out," suggests Cassie.

Emily has no problem parking, and they walk up the ramp, overwhelmed by the smell of boardwalk fries and funnel cake. Maggie wonders if those aromas fade in the dead of winter. As they walk past hotels and seafood restaurants, Cassie sees a giant seaside slide that inspires her. One by one the others drift to the railing by the ocean and gaze. Cassie is the last to join them and casually mentions, "When I was in college, we always did a team building activity before a big game."

"What did you have in mind, Captain?" asks Emily.

Cassie points in a southern direction. "See that slide?"

"The one that's three stories high and probably manned by a bunch of stoned teenagers?" asks Maggie.

"Well, yeah!"

The girls take off as Maggie lags behind. Emily doubles back. "What's wrong?"

Maggie sighs. "I'm afraid of heights. Not all heights, just out in the open, no walls around me, three-stories-up kind of heights."

"You know what, Maggie? I think most people are afraid of stuff they don't really understand," soothes Emily. Maggie thinks, *She must be the best mother on earth with that voice.* "Let's keep walking and I'll break it down. If you still don't want to do it, I've got your back."

"That's fair."

As Emily divulges the principles behind Newton's first law of motion, Maggie's mind wanders to Sean's next three questions. She never was any good at science anyway. Suddenly Maggie and Emily have entered the Seaside Slide-capades only to be handed very thin rugs from Cassie. Maggie counts the rows, five across. Shit!

"Listen to me, take the lane closest to where we enter," encourages Emily. "And I will be right next to you." Maggie returns a weak smile.

After climbing the stairs, Laci is off like a shot to the furthest lane. Jen follows suit, then Cassie. Emily gives Maggie a thumbs-up and says, "Let's go, Maggie, we only live once!"

Damn straight, thinks Maggie. This is no corporate box at an Eagles away game but a thrill nonetheless.

Maggie wiggles onto her rug and scootches up to the edge of the slide, heart pounding. The operator calls out, "Here we go, ladies. Smile for the photo op at the end." A padded bar touches their backs with a push, and they're off, gliding, laughing, screaming over each crest.

Laci is the first to pop up. "I think I got air!"

"Can we go again, Mom?" asks Jen.

Emily offers Maggie a hand up. "You did it!" Maggie gives her a hug, and Emily whispers, "Don't be afraid, Maggie. Do what you have to do to understand him and go for it if you are interested. You only live once. Now might be your chance at something special or at least some fun."

Maggie doesn't completely disagree. She stops by the checkout desk, buys the photo, and slides it into her bag.

After a triumphant order of Boardwalk fries, the girls turn around toward the car when they see Danny heading out of the Atlantic Sands Hotel donned in a pair of skinny jeans and fur vest, no shirt. Laci runs ahead and jumps him from behind. "We've been looking all over for you," she feigns. "Where you been, sunshine?"

They are huddled together over a phone screen, heads nodding in agreement as the girls catch up. Laci and Danny lay out the plans for their Friday night. Dinner back at the house, bonfire at Henolopen Park at eight, back to town to hit Darby's for open mic night.

Ping. Maggie walks away from the group.

Lunch rush over, what r u up to?

Not much, conquering my fear of heights and making a game plan for tonight. That's Q1...next please.

Whoa. That's fair... I guess.

I warned you to choose carefully.

Ok Q 2... Maggie sees the suspended "..." and smiles. He's choosing carefully.

Are you a lawyer?

Hell NO!!!! ED NPO, low income, academic advancement.

Whew, no offense u r kind of intense, very smart.

None taken and thx.

Q 3 Other than champagne what do you like to drink.

Maggie smirks as she mentally chastises him. He is so cocky, so sure she's coming in tonight. Who is she kidding? She is.

Guinness, tequila and wine but not in that order.

I would hope not.

Maggie smiles, closes the text, and puts her phone back in her pocket as she rejoins the group. This time Danny is the first to inquire, "Was that Sean?" Jen tries to give him the universally recognized slashed throat sign to not go there, but Danny ignores her and says, "Well..."

Maggie glares at Danny and says, "They didn't warn you about me, did they?"

"I'm still waiting," sings Danny.

"Well, let me both indulge and enlighten you for the one and only time I'm inclined to do so. That was my son Patrick," she lies before telling the God's honest truth, "and I'm not just some stupid bitch, I'm an alpha bitch, and if you don't watch yourself, I'll rip your balls off and serve them to the seagulls. So mind your own business and you and I will be friends. Comprendo?"

Danny to turns to Laci and says, "OMG, she's fabulous!"

"We know," replies Laci with a grin.

Once back at the house, the women naturally divide tasks by their strengths, or as Cassie put it, "Let the crafters craft, the cooks cook, and I will run cocktails." Emily brings the white garment bag, a teal-green toolbox, and the Walmart stash up from her SUV. Maggie, Jen, and Cassie bring out chips, guacamole, salsa, chilled bottles of Carona Light, limes, and skinny girl margaritas to the table. Jen drags the cooler tableside to pop the Coronas in and then pulls out a bottle of sauvignon blanc.

Danny surveys the materials and replies, "We can work with this…definitely work with this. What's our vision here, ladies?" As Laci and Emily fill him in, he looks out toward the dunes, unraveling the tulle, nodding his head, and commanding, "Tape measure, please."

Emily digs in her box and hands over the tape measure. "All right, ladies, line up, I need your waist measurements." That statement is met with a groan, to which he snaps his fingers and replies, "Suck it up! If I can dress twelve drag queens in thirty minutes, I can make you the uniform of your dreams. But you have to work with me here!"

Maggie quips, "Alpha bitch in training, nice!" She's first in line to get measured and waves on the others. A buzzer rings, and Jen disappears for a few minutes. She returns with a tray of mini chicken tacos as Danny grabs one. He pours himself another Skinny Girl Margarita and asks, "What's in the garment bag?"

Laci gives him one of her most radiant smiles and says, "The Holy Grail, Danny, to be shared with only a few." With that, Laci unzips the bag and begins pulling garments from it, laying them on the deck railing for display. There's sequined and tulle prom dresses, Alexa Karrington jackets, a fifties satin jacket, a nineties business suits, a purple satin bridesmaids dress, a pinstriped jumpsuit, and

LAST NIGHT AT DARBY'S

under it all, glistening in the seaside sun, her wedding dress and veil. She stands back and proudly offers her best Vanna White display wave.

Danny is speechless for a moment, then slowly walks over to her, genuflects, and says, "You are my sister from another mister. If you were a man, we'd be married tonight!"

Pop! Emily has started case number 2. "What's a wedding without champagne?"

Danny gets them all back on task, and thirty minutes later the tutus are completed. He instructs the women to wear bathing suits, leggings, and tutus, positively no T-shirts. He will handle their hair, accessories, and makeup and tells them wardrobe call is for ten thirty tomorrow morning to allow them time to get to the beach.

All uniforms go into the girls' rooms, and Danny eyes the wedding gown one more time, touching it respectfully, lifting the tiara and veil for closer inspection. Laci wanders onto the deck, grabs a bottle of champagne from the cooler, and asks, "Do you like it, Danny?"

"It's beautiful. Was it the happiest day of your life?"

"One of them, that and the birth of my children."

"I'll never have either of those." Danny's eyes well up, and Laci's heart breaks.

"Do you want to try it on?"

Before she can give some instructions, Danny grabs her hand, the veil, and dress and leads her back to the master bedroom, where Emily is hanging up her tutu. Together the women get Danny into the slip, strapless bra, and gown. Danny goes to the mirror, eyes himself, and asks for six bobby pins. He begins twisting his hair is into an elegant chignon, and Laci brings over the tiara, tears in her eyes, and places it on his head.

Emily says, "Wait here…just wait."

She runs out to the dining room and gathers the others, explaining the emotional moment Danny is having in her bedroom. They women quickly grasp how significant weddings are to the gay community and quickly create impromptu signs. Jen cues the music

53

as Emily calls down the short hallway, "When you hear the intro, come out, you two."

Danny and Laci walk the runway as they hear Cher start to whisper, "After love, after love, after love." They hit the center of the open space of the great room to see the women flip the signs that are holding that say "Legalize Same-Sex Marriage Now!" in rainbow markers as Cher continues to belt out "Do You Believe in Life After Love?" All begin dancing with the bride.

Danny catches his breath. "Okay, maybe it's the dress," starts Danny, "but, Laci, will you dance in the drag show with me?"

Laci needs no time to think about her reply, "Oh my god, yes! This is better than a marriage proposal! Do not tell Dex I said that. Wait, who gets to wear the dress?"

"I do! I mean, I'm sure you look great in it, but please, this A-line and my silhouette? Besides, I thought we'd make you into a hot little groom and have the girls come on stage as our bridesmaids."

They each jump on the chance, "We're in!"

Dancing ensues until the sun sets, and suddenly Jen says, "Hey, we have to get ready to go out. The bonfire begins in an hour. Danny, you are coming with us tonight, right? You are our official coach now, after all."

"I'd love to, but I don't have a *thing* to wear."

"Come on, I'll hook you up," says Laci.

An hour later, they begin to immerge from their rooms warmly dressed in layers to go from the bonfire to the bars, hair styled, makeup on. Danny and Laci are in nearly matching outfits, Jen in a shade of green that brings out her eyes, Emily in a soft peach, and Cassie in a chambray shirt and plaid wrap. "What's the holdup with Maggie?" asks Cassie.

"Wait for it," instructs Jen.

Maggie emerges from the hallway in dark wash boot cut jeans, black raw silk blouse open just enough to reveal a black lace camisole, black booties, and a red cape draped over her forearm. Her makeup is flawless, hair straightened, and artisan earrings and bracelet carefully selected. The women smile in admiration of the senior stateswoman, and Danny's jaw drops open. After a moment, he says, "Sean is in deep trouble tonight. Girl, you are wearing do-me jeans!"

Maggie rolls her eyes and says, "He should be so lucky. Let's go, we have a fire to catch."

"Or start," whispers Cassie to Jen.

CHAPTER 9

Blindsided

Emily offered to act as the designated driver for the night, intending to keep an eye on Maggie and clearly communicate with Sean, given the chance. As they enter Henolopen State Park, Danny tells her to pull into the lot on the left. The women smell the fire as they step out of the SUV. They hurriedly gather blankets and thermal bag with beverages, scurrying past the fire truck, across the street to the beach bath.

A young man with glow sticks is collecting a pay-what-you-will fee for wetlands preservation at the entrance to the beach. Maggie digs into her jeans and hands over two fifty-dollar bills and grabs a few extra glow sticks. Laci takes her glow stick and fashions herself a halo, repeating for others as they make their way to the fire. Someone has brought a decent speaker and Van Morrison's "Moondance" waffles out in their direction.

The fire is at least five feet tall, emanating warmth and a beautiful glow on the beach this chilly night. Children are dancing around the fire, bringing a smile to Maggie's face, young couples are canoodling, and adults are acting like children toasting marshmallows and sipping their solo cups. Danny points to a place to set up as Maggie thinks she spots Rosie with three men. Maggie quickly tells Jen she will join them after she says hello to someone she knows.

"Of course you know someone… Go on." Jen moves on to explain to the others and adds for Danny's benefit, "Watch and learn, grasshopper. She will have half the crowd following us in an hour. When she chooses, she's charisma personified."

Danny observes. Maggie starts with a couple with little girls, handing them the extra glow sticks. She works her way into a group of gay men and looks to be modeling her outfit to high fives. Danny strains to see who she is talking to but cannot clearly see through the flames. "Hmm," he says to the group, "this keeps up, and tonight at Darby's is going to be quite a show."

"Oh, she doesn't sing, like ever," informs Cassie.

"I'm not worried about her singing. I'm thinking someone else might sing."

"Who?" they beg. Danny withholds and slowly edges to a better vantage point fascinated by the woman who has captivated Sean, a feat previously thought of as impossible. Suddenly Rosie breaks free of her caretakers and gallops in Maggie's direction as people scatter out of the dog's way. Danny swears he hears Maggie's laughter when she turns and crouches as Rosie clumsily knocks her over with kisses.

One of the older men offers Maggie a hand, and she offers Rosie's lead back to him. As her friends move to join her, the lead remains in Maggie's hands, as she soothes Rosie by stroking her shoulders. "Hey, guys, come over here," she calls as she sees her friends approaching.

"The fine gentlemen to my right are from DC, here for a bachelor squared party," explains Maggie. She holds her hand in front of her eyes, blocking the smoke, and continues, "Rick, Jay, come on over. Their commitment ceremony is in Ohio at Rick's parents' house in two weeks. Isn't that nice?'

Congratulations begin, many wedding details exchanged. Danny sidles up next to Maggie and whispers, "Do you know who you are talking to?" She gives him an annoyed look and turns back to the older men. "Jim, I'm sorry, I couldn't hear your introductions." She holds out her hand to the man with the black knit cap. "Maggie Burke," she offers.

"Scott Perkins." Maggie picks up a faded British accent as he takes her hand and kisses it. She beams at him, and he introduces his partner, Larry.

"I'm so happy to see you, dear. How did you learn about this? I thought it was just a neighborhood thing," comments Jim.

"I told her about it," Danny interjects.

"Excuse my manners, Jim, Scott, Larry. Please allow me to introduce you to my friend Danny."

Danny is now looking at her as if she has three heads. Jim extends his hand and says, "Hi, Danny, I think we've met at Sean's house when you were doing some painting for him." Danny nods but remains stymied.

Maggie quickly learns that Scott has a home in Georgetown in addition to his place on the bay in Rehoboth. He works as a fashion curator for the Smithsonian. Larry eyes Danny and snuggles a little closer to Scott. As small chat continues, Rosie lays on Maggie's feet. Jim chuckles, "You must have run into Sean and Rosie after we met on the beach this morning."

"I did. Was that this morning? I'm starting to feel like I've been here for weeks."

"It's the sea air. Welcome to Rehoboth Beach." Scott smiles.

Emily joins them in time to overhear Jim's last comment and questions, "This is the hot bitch named Rosie that you met on your walk?" With that, Jim roars. Scott and Larry join in. Danny's mouth gapes open as he tries desperately to piece this together, thinking Maggie knows Jim and now Scott Perkins. This is weird and about to get weirder.

"You know, Maggie, Darby's is a fun spot on Friday nights," divulges Scott.

"Really, we were considering popping by."

"Oh, you should!" emphasizes Scott.

Maggie turns to Jim. "Any chance we can get you to come by for a bit?"

"Well, Scott and Larry were kind enough to include me when they picked up Rosie for a little exercise. I suppose I could stay for a set or two, but ten thirty is my curfew."

"Us too," says Scott.

"It's settled then." Maggie leans in and gives Jim a kiss and a hug before handing over Rosie's lead to Larry. She bends down, takes Rosie's head in her hands, and says, "You be a good girl and go home and get to bed."

She turns and after a few steps whips her cape around her shoulders like a matador and heads for the blankets and wine. Jen looks at Danny and says, "And that's how it's done."

Cassie comes over. "The DC guys are coming to Darby's." Jen and Emily give Danny a glance that reads "I told you so."

After a bottle of champagne, they make their way back to the car. Maggie glances to her left to scan the crowd, glad to see Jim has made his way off the beach safely, hoping to see him as promised.

She wonders why Scott is so familiar. She must have seen him in a photo at Sean's house. She places him at seventy, give or take. Danny gives directions from the front passenger seat, and Maggie spies Dogfish brewery on the left. Her mind goes to his hat from the beach when she first met him, yesterday. She snaps out of her daydream as Emily makes a soft left and parks about five hundred feet from the little restaurant they just passed with a small illuminated sign, Darby's Café, All Welcome. *Deep breaths*, thinks Maggie, *deep breaths*.

Danny turns around and hands Maggie a small lit mirror. "Check those lips, Maggie."

She promptly swats his hand, sending the little mirror flying. She feels the air closing in on her inside the car and nearly jumps out of the Tahoe. No need for a mirror, she swipes the clear gloss of her lip stain as she walks to the front door at a brisk pace.

Laci holds Danny back. Cassie catches up with Maggie and says, "Last, Maggie, you enter last." She straightens her cape, and Maggie glares. "For the love of God, they paid less attention to my looks on my wedding day. Leave me alone."

The self-appointed entourage hurry past her, and Maggie exhales, thinking that the little blast of temper felt pretty darn good. She thinks to herself, *Let's do this*.

She opens the door to a hum of conversation and music. The site of a long wooden bar filled with patrons sitting on cherrywood barstools warms her heart. The wide planked hardwood floors have integrity, unlike the newly manufactured floors with complete symmetry to them. The lighting is low but manageable. Her father's voice is in her head, "Your guests have to see each other and the surroundings to feel at home before you even welcome them."

As she scans down the bar, she sees the Guinness tap. She wonders if she should just stick her head under it and let it flow until her nerves calm. As she gazes past the tap, she sees Jim with a spot at the end of the bar, Scott and Larry behind him. Beyond that a dining room. As she walks toward the center of the bar, a large open archway leads to a room on the left filled with high and low tops, stage, instruments, and open space. She thinks, *Hmm, dancing.*

Sean is back farther toward the right in a smaller dining room finishing some notes for later in the evening. As Maggie opened the front door, he made his way toward the bar, happy to see Scott, Larry, and Jim. He stops to thank them for coming in, explaining that he will catch up with them in a few, but quickly asking if Rosie was any trouble. Larry reports, "Not unless you count knocking Maggie on her ass on the beach at the bonfire a problem."

Sean shakes his head as he ducks under the service bar. Maggie finds an open barstool three seats past the beer taps, and as she begins to sit down, who pops up from the service entrance of the bar but, what did Jen call him, tall dark, and edgy. With that thought in mind, she relaxes and gives him a reassuring smile. He places his hands on the bar top and casually leans in her direction, "Welcome, Maggie, what can I get you?"

"Umm, I think I need to order more than a few drinks, but I don't see my friends."

"I took their orders. They went to the ladies' room." He nods to his left. "Jesse's on it." Maggie sees five cranberry and vodkas in process. "We have a table reserved for you over there on the right." He leans in closer to her and points. She turns to gaze in that direction. Her hair is inches from him. He takes in a heady mixed aroma of firewood and roses. He comments, "How was the bonfire?"

"Beautiful, actually, what a nice community event." Her mind tells her she sounds like she is eighty years old. *Smooth, very smooth there, girl.*

Rather than bait her, he openly apologizes, "I heard Rosie was not exactly well behaved. I'm sorry. You okay?"

She smiles. "My fault, I crouched down too soon. And I would hope I didn't get hurt falling on the sand. I'm not that old!"

Jesse slides the cranberry and vodkas Sean's way as her friends return. Maggie helps pass them back and gives Jen a "beat it" look. Jen quickly connects, "Thanks, Sean."

He invites Jen to take the reserved table before someone else does. "All right, miss, your drink order please." Maggie eyes the Guinness tap and thinks, *Later.* She considers red wine but already feels warm and begins to remove her cape. At the sight of the black silk blouse and lace camisole, Sean steps back, reaches onto the shelf without turning around, and pulls a bottle of Patron without ever taking his eyes off her.

He places the Patron on the bar top, and she responds, "That'll work."

Sean pulls two shot glasses and a small rocks glass on top of the bar. "Salt? Lime?"

"Nope."

He leans in again close enough to take in that aroma, sets his dark gaze on her, and says, "Maggie, you fascinate the hell out of me."

He fills both shots, free-pours two fingers into the old fashion, sends one shot in her direction, and holds her gaze as they unceremoniously take the first down the proverbial hatch. He fills a second old fashion glass with ice and squeezes two limes over it before sliding both in her direction. "Just in case you want a little seasoned ice with the next one," he says.

Maggie thanks him and pulls fifty dollars from her pants pocket. He scolds her and says, "Put that away. I invited you here." Maggie thinks of her father again. He would fire a bartender for that.

"Look, I've got a few things to take care of before it gets too crowded. Please stay until I can talk to you."

Maggie thinks, *Okay, not bartender...manager... Whatever, his job is not important to her*, and says, "Sure."

Sean ducks back under the service bar, and Maggie waves Jesse over. She pulls the fifty dollars out of her pocket and says, "Hey, Jesse, my friends are guaranteed to be a handful tonight, so I'm tipping you now."

"Sorry, Maggie, no can do. He'll fire my ass."

She gives him a perplexed look and picks up her tequila and rocks to go talk to Scott and Larry. She feels the need to connect some dots. The crowd is steadily filling in as the musicians begin messing around on stage. As she turns the corner of the bar, she sees Sean talking to a sweet strawberry blonde but tries not to stare. Before she can reach Scott and Larry, the little blonde walks up to her and says, "Hi, Maggie, I'm Becca. Sean would like me to take your cape and clutch back to his office so they don't get ruined."

Again, Maggie is confused. "Umm, okay?" and as she hands them over, Becca says, "Jesse or I can get them for you anytime you need them."

Maggie looks to her left and sees shot glasses and the DC boys filling her friends' table. She sips her tequila, putting the ice back on the bar, and makes her way to Jim and Scott and Larry. The band is tuning up. Maggie asks Scott, "What time is it?"

"Nine forty-five, why?"

"What goes down here tonight?"

"Well, the band will warm up with an instrumental or two. You know, James Taylor, Cat Stevens, that kind of thing. Then a regular might get up and get things rolling, it just takes off from there. However, sometimes, someone extremely talented shows up, and it's magical. The first person Sean brought in was Bonnie Raitt. That was surreal."

"What?"

"Yeah, and he's had a plenty of others. The Hooters, not my favorites but people went nuts, Tom Petty, but the night Patti Scialfa and Nils Lofgren showed up really cemented this place as a permanent fixture in Rehoboth."

"I repeat, what?" Her mind races, *Who the hell is this guy?*

Jim takes her glass, places it on the bar, and says, "Come with me, Maggie." He walks her into the little dining room and stops in front of a photograph near the entrance to a garden terrace. He points to the couple. "Do you know who these people are?"

"I think the younger man looks like he could be Sean's brother, and I guess that's his partner."

"You guessed correctly. His brother was Tony DeMarco, and Tony's partner was Edwin Darby." Jim then pulled her into the garden. "Watch your step, young lady." They walked hand in hand to an abstract fountain. "This was one of Tony's works."

Maggie feels drawn to the piece but remains on task. "Jim, I'm confused. I mean, I think I know what happened, but I have so many questions."

"Maggie, it's not my story to tell, but I was here for all of it. Trust him. I know he wants to tell it to you. He's a good man, one of the best I've known. Now, honey, let's go back in because it's cold out here."

Feeling reassured, she pecks Jim on the cheek and leads the way back inside to crowded restaurant. By that time, someone had begun singing "Up on a Roof." A nervous young black woman is pacing to the left of the stage, presumably up next. A seat has opened up by the service bar, and Maggie insists that Jim sit down. She then grabs her tequila and downs it in a weak attempt to calm her growing nerves.

Emily is speaking to Scott, nodding her head in an understanding way. Maggie thinks, *Something tells me that is not a fashion consultation.* She sees Jen and Cassie laughing with the DC party, a fresh order of cocktails delivered via Jesse. She peers into the stage area and sees Laci, Danny, and Larry working on dance moves.

The young woman takes the stage, and the band begins a familiar intro, but Maggie can't place it. Probably because she is losing her mind, she thinks.

The singer begins, and after the first few notes, the boisterous bar is silent.

> You got a fast car,
> I want a ticket to anywhere,
> Maybe we make a deal
> Maybe together we can get somewhere.

Maggie scans for Sean, sees him schmoozing tables, and as if he realized she was looking at him, he lifts his head so that those eyes burn through her from across the room. She looks away, struggling to breathe. Becca is handing slips of paper out at the tables. Maggie needs water. She tries to get Jesse's attention but sees him slammed behind the bar. Scott and Emily come up behind her, causing her to practically jump out of her skin. "Maggie, Emily here should be your PR person. I'd like to hear more about your work with your students sometime."

"Thank you, Scott, it's really all them. And Em is a little biased about me, only believe half of it…the good and the bad."

Social norms, all will be okay…breathe, she tells herself. She eyes the garden door and strategizes how to go over the wall without getting caught by her friends. She turns to Emily and Scott and excuses herself to find the ladies' room. She makes it to the garden, and her head begins to clear with each breath. The wall is made of fieldstone, about five feet high. If she could move one of the wrought iron chairs over without drawing any attention, she could clear it, but she does not have her purse. This is a problem.

She decides instead to try to sort through this, at least for now. Sean's brother and his partner are no longer with us, AIDS epidemic. She feels her heart constrict. Patrick. Next, there is a bar in Edwin's memory? Sean manages it—owns it? What is she doing? Why is she here?

She gazes up at the brilliant stars, finds little solace, and as she hears his steps, she thinks she should have scaled the wall while she had the chance.

"Hey, you aren't thinking about going AWOL on me, are you?"

She turns. "Maybe we should do this another time."

"When are you leaving?"

"Monday."

He steps inside her personal space and calmly says, "Look, I committed to something a month ago. Let me see it through, and I'll be free in less than thirty minutes. Can you hang in?" And as he asks her the question, his right hand is caressing her hair below her jawline, and he lets his thumb barely brush her cheek. His touch reassures her of some sort of connection while simultaneously unnerving her to her core.

"I'll try," she offers.

"Try hard," he responds. He gently guides her back to the bar, and she sees that Jim is now sitting with Jen and Cassie. Becca walks up to Sean and says, "You ready?"

"Does Jesse have backup?" Becca nods at two waiters coming from the kitchen. Scott puts an arm around Maggie and tells Sean, "I've got this one, go on."

Sean says to Maggie, "See you in twenty…thirty tops." She thought he was going to kiss her, but Scott is moving her toward Emily and Jen with the elegance of a ballroom dancer midwaltz. Jen and Cassie yell, "Maggie! Where have you been, girl?" She feels their support and settles in ready to see the next courageous singer.

The drummer is stretching the time as pink papers find their way to a basket on the floor. A recording of "Sweet Home Alabama" is playing, the crowd is starting to sing the refrain, and Maggie's foot is tapping. Maggie hears a woman say, "Is he really playing tonight? He never plays anymore."

A busboy brings a beautiful guitar on stage, and the crowd starts clapping. The other musicians come back on stage, and at the end of the line is Sean DeMarco. She thinks, *What?*

Emily says it first, "Oh my god, Sean is going to sing!" Jen and Cassie are whooping, Laci is jumping up and down in front of the stage, and all Maggie can think is *What the hell? I did not see this coming.*

Scott leans in and says to Maggie, "Enjoy it, sweetie. He's got a great voice."

Sean places the guitar strap over his head and steps to the microphone. "Hey, everyone, I'm Sean DeMarco." The crowd erupts. "I don't do this much anymore, but a month ago a friend of mine was in a pretty bad accident, and I told him I'd play again if he'd only get his ass out of the hospital." A pair of crutches waves at him from the left side of the room. The crowd cheers.

Sean starts strumming, trying to get adjusted. He looks back at the drummer, left and right, and says, "I used to set up shows for the guy that wrote this song. Don't leave me hangin', join in." With that, Sean opens with "Take it Easy," and the crowd is carrying the refrain.

Maggie is in shock over the whiskey-throated baritone singing in front of her.

Sean stoops to pick up a pink Post-it note, turns to his band members, and starts again. Maggie knows the song immediately, and "Melissa" fills the room. A tough ballad, she thinks. And Sean does not have lyrics in front of him, when the guitar solo comes at the end, she almost cries from the emotional pull of the song. Sean wishes the couple a happy anniversary and intros the next song.

"For some reason life can put us through the wringer, and when it was my time to move through hell, there was a couple that lived next door to me that pulled me through just by being who they were together. This song goes out to Jim and Eileen. I miss you, sweetie." As "Never Die Young" begins, Jim stands and blows a kiss toward heaven.

Maggie waits for the song to end and goes over to Jim. He turns to her and says, "Maggie, you know that feeling you have like you're about to have a panic attack?" She nods her agreement. "Well, dear, that's called meeting your match." She beams at him and kisses him for the third time that night.

Sean moves through two more numbers then starts to remove his guitar. The crowd has caught on, and someone near Maggie yells, "Bruce!" Maggie is almost sick. That is an impossible request. The guitar stays put. Sean scans the audience as the drummer starts beating. "Mac, Jesse, get your asses up here." Becca scoots past Maggie carrying a sax, Jesse right behind her. Mac meets them down stage, and Becca gives Mac a huge kiss, marking her territory.

The Bruce chants continue until Jesse has his bass guitar plugged in and Mac waves the sax at Sean. A band member picks up a fiddle as Sean starts strumming and approaches the mic. "Forgive me, Father, for I have sinned." Again, the crowd erupts as he begins "Waiting on a Sunny Day." When Mac takes the lead on the saxophone, Maggie smiles at Becca. Sean continues, "Without you, I'm working with the rain fallin' down." He is having a blast moving through the lyrics before he gets everyone to sing the final refrain and waves Jesse over and says, "I'm getting too old for this."

He places his guitar on a stand, salutes his friend in the back, and ducks to the right. Maggie moves while the band is still playing, and her friends remain captivated by the music. Maggie heads for the garden, the cool air focusing her thoughts but not her emotions. Where to start? Sean appears, dishrag around his neck and a sheepish look on his face. She takes full advantage and snaps at him, "Exactly who has been holding out on whom?"

"Maggie, I know, it's a lot."

"A lot… I thought I was losing my mind an hour ago, thanks for that. I can't put this together, and it is freaking me out. Who the hell are you?"

He walks toward her, holds out his hand, and says, "Take my hand and come with me." She recoils, shaking her head no. He steps closer. "Just come to my office for a few minutes."

As Maggie reluctantly follows, Sean grabs a pitcher of water and pours two glasses from a wait station, offering one to Maggie. He unlocks the white door that Maggie has passed three or four times tonight. The room is charcoal-gray hardwood floors. There are two desks, one rather small. The other is a farm table, no drawers, with a narrow credenza behind it holding a few picture frames and a lot of paperwork. A leather sofa hugs the right wall, Maggie's cape and clutch tucked on one end.

Anxiety is rearing up in Maggie. Sean finishes his water and says, "Let's just leave the music out of it for a minute."

Before he can finish his sentence, she pounces, "Leave it out? Okay, let's leave out the restaurant too. What else can we leave out? I mean, what am I doing in here with you, Sean?"

"We are trying to have a conversation, Maggie, that's all."

"Great, let's talk." Sean is trying to get a read on her and hangs back. She steps toward him, eyes completely electrified with anger. "You know what? I do have a few questions. Is this your office? Like do you own this place?" she peppers.

"Affirmative."

"Hold up, that's not enough of an answer. How? When? And why when you can sing and play guitar like that?"

"You're overloading the questions, Maggie, which leaves me no choice but to ask you to come home with me so I can tell you the whole story."

"Hit the Pause button on that one, Sean. I've got one more, and I want it answered right now. How sexually active are you? Like, you must get laid all the time with that talent of yours." She puts her hands over her face, and he hears her say, "Oh my god, what am I doing?"

"You really suck at asking questions, you know that, Maggie? Ask, then shut up and let me answer." He studies her intently and sees a few less lightning bolts coming at him.

"First of all, I haven't been active in way too long. You want to do a medical check on me, ask the drummer, he's my doc. Secondly, what you, or shall I say we, are trying to do is figure out if this is a, a harmless flirtation, it's not, b, a magnetically charged sexual attraction, it is, and c, if there is any shot at creating something more in the next forty-eight hours, personally I'd like to know."

Maggie narrows her eyes and starts pacing. She hates reason. This has nothing to do with reason.

"What are you afraid of, Maggie?"

"I'm afraid of you, Sean, I'm very afraid of you. Help me understand you, this, all of it."

"Come home with me, Maggie. We need time together."

Becca wraps on the door and peeks in. "I'm sorry, boss. Pedro's getting ready to head out."

He drills into Maggie. "Don't move. Becca, stay here, she's a flight risk. This will take two minutes."

Becca explains that Sean is saying goodbye to a seasonal employee who has taken a new job in Wilmington for the winter. Maggie nods, head swirling. Becca says, "Maggie, sit down, you're making me nervous."

"I'm okay…" She walks toward a photo of Sean's brother and absentmindedly asks, "Is the drummer really a doctor?"

"Yup, Sean goes to him, Mac and I do too. Why, do you not feel well? I'll go get him when Sean comes back."

"No, that's okay." Maggie moves behind the desk. She stares at a small photo on Sean's desk from the early seventies. It shows a pretty woman with auburn hair, her arms around two boys on a front stoop, one a teenager with long wavy hair, wooden beads, and a buckskin jacket, and the other is a boy with chestnut curls and a baseball jersey. She muses to herself, *That little guy has a bad attitude. His poor mother.*

Sean walks in with a tray holding a freshly poured Guinness. He thanks Becca, and she exits as fast as her legs can carry her. He notices Maggie looking at his boyhood photo but refuses to comment. He places the tray on the table, and Maggie accepts the peace offering.

"I'm saying the same thing you are, Maggie, just differently. I'd like to know you better because this attraction, in this small town, with this short of a timeline is only going to lead to one place…my bedroom."

Maggie sips her Guinness, refusing to make this easy on him, all the while knowing that she, too, is to blame for some of the tension. She narrows her eyes in his direction. "Don't be so sure of that, Sean. I'm pretty confident I drive the outcome here."

She walks away from the desk toward Sean. She holds an intense gaze his way. He makes his best attempt at defusing the situation by saying, "Look, you can't deny the chemistry. I am not trying to hide anything, Maggie. I would like to spend some time with you."

Maggie thinks about their coffee this morning, the drop-off, the nice text messages throughout the day, and quietly says, "All right, Sean, I'll go with you." He retrieves her cape and gently places it on her shoulders, and as she turns around to face him, he brings her to him and kisses her, and her anxiety dissipates. She tilts her head with a request, "Sneak me out the back door…please, Sean."

"Way ahead of you, Maggie, way ahead of you."

As they exit the kitchen, Maggie sees the Jeep idling, roof on, and thinks that Sean DeMarco is indeed way ahead of her.

CHAPTER 10

True Depth of a Man

Instead of watching the road, Maggie's eyes are on Sean. She makes no attempt at small talk and is completely comfortable in the silence during the short drive to his home. Sean parks the Jeep in front of the garage door and once again walks around to open her door, leaving Maggie to wonder, did she actually wait for it this time? Walking toward his front steps, he pauses, points to the next house closest to the beach, and says, "That's Jim's house."

Maggie smiles. "Good night, Jim," she says and blows a kiss, adding, "Sweet dreams."

Rosie barks as he unlocks the door. "Hey, girl, it's me," Sean announces. Rosie appears down the steps, sees Maggie, and begins to get excited. Sean's voice lowers an octave, "Behave." The dog immediately sits by his left side. He pats her head and says, "Good girl."

Once inside, they head straight to the kitchen. The back of the house has an anterior room with a wall of windows. There is no dining table, only barstools on the opposite side of a granite top island. Maggie thinks, *No children,* as she deposits her cape and clutch.

Sean tosses keys into a hammered pewter dish and says, "Wine? Water?"

"Water, please."

He walks into the anterior room, opens the flue, and lights the premade fire. She takes her water and steps down into the anterior room. "I'm going to take a quick shower to get the grime of the day off of me. Make yourself at home."

She asks, "Did you stop and eat today?"

"Not a chance."

"You shower. I'll make you a sandwich or something." He smiles in appreciation, heads up the stairs, and yells down, "Thanks. Take your boots off, woman, you're gonna be here awhile."

Maggie rummages through the refrigerator for ingredients, hunts for bread, and scans the freezer. *We have an ice cream habit*, she notes. He returns in fresh jeans, a damn fine Henley, and bare feet. He eyes the turkey, sharp provolone, and arugula sandwich, disappears to the front room, and returns with a bottle of red wine, which he promptly opens, grabs two glasses from the wine rack, and places them on the coffee table between the fireplace and couch.

Maggie brings him the sandwich. She returns to the kitchen, and he asks, "Where are you going?" He's about to move to rejoin her in the kitchen when she appears with two bowls of rocky road ice cream garnished with thin salty pretzels.

She places the bowls on the coffee table, selects the end of the couch with the mohair throw, and bends down to remove her boots before curling up, ice cream in hand. "Eat," she instructs, "before your ice cream melts."

As Sean devours his sandwich, Maggie reveals, "I was a restaurant rug rat. My dad owned a tavern in Ardmore, and we all pretty much grew up there. When I got older and would work until closing with him, we kind of had a tradition to come home, grab a sandwich, some ice cream, and talk politics or events of the day until he fell asleep in his recliner."

"How many is *we*?"

"I was sixth out of seven. Three boys, four girls, six college educated, courtesy O'Rourke's Tavern."

"Dad's name?"

"Marty. He was a hardworking man with a social conscientious. A total badass with a heart of gold."

Sean responds, "Clearly, look at his offspring." This earns him a smile.

71

He stands up, tops off both of their wineglasses, picks up the ice cream, and lands back on his end of the couch to face her dead-on. "I think we should put a little structure on this. Otherwise we could end up down a rabbit hole."

"You're driving this bus, go ahead."

"Hmm... I feel like I owe you somewhat of an explanation."

"Ah, yeah, you do!"

"All right, but you have to let me get it out." He pauses to assess her and continues, "There's no other way to do this, so I'm going to have to ask you to let me pause before you start with questions. Deal?"

"I'll try."

"How about a yes, Maggie, just once."

"Nope, I'm saving that for later, or it wouldn't be special."

"And none of that before you've had your turn at this too."

"None of what?"

"The sparring, the verbal foreplay, the challenges laced with seduction."

She stretches her legs toward him and says, "Fine, but you're taking all the fun out of it."

"Just for now, woman. I'm sure we'll manage to pick right up where we've left off later."

With that, Sean launches into his background. A tough kid born into a tougher neighborhood in Trenton. His dad left his mother, Mary Doyle DeMarco, when he was four years old and never resurfaced. His mother once told him she knew she was going to have to raise him on her own, so she chose the most Irish name she could think of before leaving the hospital. They lived in a two-bedroom row home. Mom worked at the diner down the street. She was a strong-willed woman determined to remain independent.

His brother, Tony, was his best friend. He was smart, creative, and patient with Sean. Tony's humor was infectious, and he emerged as a popular teen in the neighborhood. Tony graduated with honors from the Philadelphia Art Institute and moved to NYC in 1973. When Sean was about ten years old, his mother sat him down to try and explain how his brother was different from Sean.

"I'm pretty sure I said something like, 'Yeah, Ma, I know Tony's gay.'"

Maggie thinks of her girls and offers, "It's that simple for kids, isn't it? We instill love in them, and they instill it in each other." Sean looks for more from her, but she is in listening mode, so he goes on.

"I was pretty good at math and obsessed with rock 'n' roll. A music teacher in high school told me the best musicians were mathematically inclined. She and her husband went to our church, and I struck a deal that if I sang in the choir, she would get me a guitar and teach me how to play."

Sean talks about his decision go to Drexel to study acoustical engineering. He didn't want to be a performer because the odds for success were too great and he knew what being poor tasted like. Bitter. Sound technology was changing quickly, and he felt he was at the epicenter of it. He worked as a crewmember at venues like the Mann, the Tower, the Keswick, and eventually the Spectrum. He would pick up and play in bands whenever and wherever he could for extra cash.

At age thirty, Tony was happily living as an openly gay man in the Village. He had begun a serious relationship with a man twenty years his senior, a Broadway costume designer, Edwin Darby. Edwin adored Tony and stepped in to do a little mentoring with Sean.

Edwin famously sued the producers of *Dream Girls* over the artistic rights to the costumes and won a huge settlement, including royalties. AIDS was on the rise, but Edwin and Tony were in a committed relationship and feeling secure. Edwin wanted to invest in a beach property but wanted nothing to do with Fire Island. They bought in Rehoboth.

Maggie asks, "Are we sitting in their house?" Sean nods yes.

By 1983, Sean was a young sought-after sound engineer, having signed contracts with East Coast legs of national tours in '82 and '83. In January of '84, the call came. He was asked to manage the sound for the Born in the USA tour from June 29 through September 25, ending in Buffalo. The camaraderie of the band and crew was unlike anything Sean had experienced. It was just fun.

Sean continues, "Until it wasn't. In the middle of the five-night stand in Philadelphia, my mother called. Edwin was sick. Not a little sick, he was dying. I hadn't made it down here for my usual summer visit, and they didn't want to bother me. Imagine that…"

Maggie sees him drift into another place and fights to contain her emotions as she watches the pain of the statement strip away his hard exterior.

After a long pause he continues, "Well, I lost it. My mentor and brother were dead men. I put my fist through the wall in the piece-of-shit office we used at the Spectrum, smashed my soundboard, ran out onto Pattison Avenue, threw up, and started harassing anyone who dared to look at me. A Philly cop came over, ready to arrest me. My manager had followed me, and all I could do was break down and cry, right there on the sidewalk.

"Within in an hour of being booked, an attorney shows, up, gets the charges dropped, and hands me an envelope. Patti had been walking in for rehearsal and saw the cop put me in the back of his car. The envelope contained two thousand dollars in cash, a six months' severance check, and a personal note asking me to go take care of my family and myself. They each signed it, and she left their personal cell number.

"Someone had called my emergency contact, Tony, trying to figure out the trigger and shared the circumstances with Patti. Days later, Bruce called my mother to tell her we were all in their prayers."

Maggie stands up, tears streaming, arms folded around her stomach. "When did they die?"

"Edwin, December 31, 1984. Tony, June 11, 1986."

She speaks just louder than a whisper, "I need a minute…"

She walks into the front room, looks at their photo, and a sob softy escapes. He is next to her, turns her around, and envelopes her, soothing her by stroking her hair as she weeps. She turns her head against his shoulder and explains, "Sean, my son is gay. It's hard now. I can't even imagine what it was like then. I'm so sorry."

He breaks the embrace. "We need a break, and Rosie needs a short walk. Come on, it will help."

It is after one in the morning, and the streets are still. The distant rhythm of the surf and dimly moonlit streets provide the perfect setting for Sean to continue to open up to her. In the time it took to circle the block, Sean has explained that Tony bought the restaurant after Edwin died and named it after him. Tony inherited the bulk of Edwin's estate and was doing his best to squander the cash before his time ran out. In the end, Sean and his mother were Tony's primary caregivers, Mary passing six months after her son, presumably of a broken heart.

By the time Sean was twenty-nine years old, he had inherited a large portfolio, a restaurant, a home, and so on. He found himself without family or purpose. He temporarily closed the doors on the restaurant and, after two years of absentee ownership, moved into the house and struck a friendship with the Wharton professor and his wife that lived next door. Jim helped him survive, first by restoring the house then by digging into the business matters of Darby's.

Rosie heads straight upstairs as they enter the house. Maggie prods, "Now it's my turn to ask three questions. Let's finish that wine."

They settle back in, and Sean says, "Okay, let me have 'em."

"Scott said something about Patti Scialfa and Niles Lofgren showing up at Darby's. How did that happen?"

"Patti sent me a Christmas card every year. She would always write, 'Hope you are well. Let us know if you ever need anything.' In 1991, I wanted to open a shelter for the growing gay homeless population in Rehoboth Beach, so I called her. Bruce was away, but she came. She brought her kids and Niles. She and Bruce anonymously gave the lead gift to get it built."

Maggie ponders question number 2 but goes for it. "There's no mention of a serious relationship. No woman anywhere in there, Sean?"

"No, there was. I was involved with someone from '94 to 2002. She handled our PR. Let's just say it ended when my restaurant manager, girlfriend, and company bank account disappeared on the same day. Although she tried to come back."

"They always do," sighed Maggie. "So over the last twelve years…nothing?"

Sean chuckles, "No, not nothing. Lord, Maggie, I'm not celibate. You just have sexual partners, not relationships. It's very different, and I am tired of it. I didn't realize how tired until I met you."

She casts a critical eye in his direction thinking this man is a little too smooth, deciding to see if she can rattle him a bit. "Okay, I just want to know what I'm working with here." She pats the seat closest to her on the couch. "Over here, big guy, because this last one is a doozy."

"You come here."

"Happy to." Maggie stands, walks to his end of the couch, puts her arms on his shoulders, straddles him, eyes locked, and flatly asks, "Does Rosie get freaked out if the sex is noisy?"

"Not usually." He pulls the shirttails of her blouse out of her jeans and slides his hand inside her camisole, kissing her intensely while unbuttoning her blouse with the other. She is up, off his lap, and leading him upstairs. Rosie leaves the room to sleep at the top of the stairs as soon as they hit the bed.

Sean has certainly not been celibate. Maggie is fighting sleep, trying to both savor and study him in the dimly lit room. Sean's breathing indicates he is fading fast. He strokes her hair and barely whispers, "Don't go, Maggie."

She grins to herself, gently kisses his neck, and responds, "I can't, silly. I don't have my car."

He turns toward her, pulling her closer, and groggily whispers, "Please don't go." With that, he is off into REM land, leaving Maggie to comprehend that he is not referring to tonight.

CHAPTER 11

Who's on the Couch?

Eyes closed, Maggie arches her back, digging hips and shoulders into the mattress as she stretches her arms over her head, remembering with a smile what happened when she did this a few hours earlier. She looks to her right, vacancy! She sits up looking around for Rosie, gone as well.

She needs something to put on so she walks buck naked over to Sean's walk-in closet, finds a flannel shirt, and puts it on. She quickly scans his wardrobe. Two nice suits, a sport coat, a dozen or so dress shirts, and roughly fifteen pairs of jeans. Different lifestyle than Kevin. Like 180 degrees different.

In the bathroom, she hunts for a new toothbrush, finds them in the linen closet, and freshens up to the best of her ability. She makes the bed before heading downstairs, hoping to be back in it soon. She lays her jeans and silk blouse on top of the bed for the walk of shame later today.

Maggie peaks into the spare bedrooms, finding one has become an office. In it are several framed photos from major concert venues, an antique desk and chair, and two acoustic guitars, one Fender and another Gibson. Sheet music lays on an armchair. She hightails it out of there, feeling she has invaded his private space. As she heads down the steps, she thinks to herself, *Okay, so you snooped. It serves him right for leaving me here.*

Once in the kitchen, she finds a note from Sean. He and Rosie are on their morning walk. The french press is set and ready for hot water. Maggie fills the teakettle and searches for breakfast food. As she surveys the fridge again, for the second time in less than twelve hours, she determines his chef sends him home with supplies from the weekly food orders. What man really buys himself arugula?

She hears the keys in the front door and the dancing of Rosie's paws on the porch. Sean sees her as soon as he opens the door, Rosie romping toward her before heading to her water dish. "I could get used this sight when I open the door." Sean smiles. "Especially if you promise to keep wearing my shirts."

"Don't get used to it. Flannel really isn't my thing."

He eyes her legs as he deposits a pastry bag on the counter. "Well, maybe it should be."

She smells fresh scones, yum! "Why didn't you wake me? I would have loved a walk this morning."

"Well, first of all, I thought you needed your sleep. Secondly, Rosie tried her best. You really don't remember one hundred pounds jumping on the bed and kissing you?"

"Oh, I thought it was just you…again."

They are right back to where they left off, playful banter. Sean comes up behind her, leans in, arms around her, and whispers, "When it's me again, you'll remember it."

When coffee is ready, they head to the anterior room, which is already neat as pin. Sean carefully approaches the topic of spending the day together. "So other than a volleyball game, what are your obligations today?"

"Oh, geez, the volleyball game. What time is it?"

"Nine. The game isn't till one."

"Well…we have a wardrobe call at ten thirty." Maggie smiles.

"Danny?" Sean asks. Maggie nods, and he continues, "So at the risk of freaking you out, I was thinking about taking the day off today."

"Look at me, not freaked." She smiles, eyes flirtatious, and holds out her hands. "Steady as can be."

"I have a theory about some of that. I think not understanding me was only part of the problem."

Her mind flashes, *Oh, good Lord, he's analyzing me*, but she's having too much fun to worry about that. "Please enlighten me."

"I think you don't relish everyone knowing your business."

"Very astute…or am I that obvious?"

"Sorry, Maggie, it's the latter. If we go into the house together this morning, it might defuse the interrogation. Then after the game and whatever follows, we give everyone the slip, come back here, and make dinner together."

Maggie's brain sends her a signal. *Warning: he's nesting.* She takes a deep breath, thinks, *Stay ahead of him, girl,* and says, "Can you make it a day on the Harley instead of the Jeep?"

"Yes, but you have to wear a helmet."

"Oh, all right," Maggie teases with a teenage eye roll.

The dark eyes soften, and Sean says, "Still not a simple yes, but I'll take what I can get."

By ten o'clock, Maggie has showered, put on her clothes from the night before, and is ready to face the music. She steps out onto the front porch to find Jim and Sean inspecting something on the bike. Maggie heads down the steps, and Jim looks up with a smile. "Good morning, Maggie, a pleasure to see you as always." Maggie thinks Jim should give lessons to all millennial men on to how to treat a woman.

"The pleasure is mine, Jim."

Jim waves Maggie over to the bike. "You ever been on one of these before?"

"It's been a very long time, but yes."

"Well, I've given Sean a strong lecture about not going too fast since he'll have you as a passenger." Maggie smiles at Sean. "So you need to promise me something, young lady."

"Anything, Jim, name it."

"You get on this bike with him, and you lean in real close and hold him tight. Got it?"

"Got it!"

And with that, Jim turns to Sean and gives him a stage wink and whisper, "My work here is done," as he returns to his house.

Sean pulls the motorcycle behind her car at the rental property. Maggie hops off the bike and is reminded that she is not even close to eighteen anymore, which was the last time she road on the back of a motorcycle. That stunt got her promptly placed on the schedule at the Tavern for late shifts Thursday through Saturday night for two months. It was worth it then, and judging by the eyes peering over the deck, it was worth it now.

Maggie smiles back at Sean as they walk in. She puts her index finger to her lips as they begin the ascent to the second floor of the house. She wants to hear the chatter, but there is none. As they enter the second floor, they notice a body on the couch fully covered in a blanket, the displayed wedding dress, and three women holding coffee mugs on the deck. Sean pulls the door open, and they all give him a significant "Shh!"

Once fully outside, Jen starts in, "I thought we talked about this, young lady."

Cassie is next. "You are sooo grounded."

Maggie replies, "Been there, done that, same crime, 1981."

Emily shakes her head, smiling. "Your poor mother, how the hell did you raise such great kids, Maggie?"

"Simple, I put the fear of God into them. That, and I only had three. She had seven."

Sean enters the conversation. "I assume the corpse in there is Danny?"

Laci is climbing up the outside steps to the top deck. "Nope. That's Larry. I thought we were going to have to call you two for backup for a while there last night. Danny slept in my room. I slept with Cassie. Love the hog, by the way."

"Is our coach awake yet?" asks Cassie.

Laci grins. "Yeah, I told him to get his ass in the shower and blow the stink off. He's in a bitch of a mood, girls. Mimosas ready?"

"Danny is in a bitch of a mood, who'd notice?" comments Maggie.

"Whoa, this is a tough crowd. And exactly who is getting married?" asks Sean.

Jen observes that Sean has not flinched at the sight of the wedding gown. "The toughest, Sean, but something tells me you can handle it. As for the wedding gown…stay tuned."

It is soon decided that Sean should use Maggie's car to return Larry to Scott while the girls prepare for the game. Maggie's only request was that Sean not allow Larry to vomit in her car, strongly encouraging him to put the roof down in spite of the chilling temperatures. A very green Larry left with barely an audible word as Danny flew up the steps, ready to take charge.

"Move it, ladies, bathing suits, bootie shorts, or leggings, preferably all black."

"No worries on the bootie shorts," retorts Cassie.

Laci's voice comes from Emily's back bedroom, "Not so fast, Cassie." Two heartbeats later, she has taken center stage of the great room in black sequin short shorts and her electric-pink bikini top.

"That's what I'm talking about. Now go help the others with their basics while I set up for hair, makeup, and tutus." By setting up, Danny clearly meant helping himself to champagne and the fridge. Laci shoos the women back to Jen and Maggie's room.

"God, I thought we'd never be alone." With that, she hands Maggie a glass of champagne, gently pushes her onto her unslept-in bed, and says, "Spill it, sister."

That request is met with an eye roll as Maggie attempts to get up and escape. The women build a human barrier to the door. Laci continues, "You're wasting time. Don't make me water board your ass, because I will."

"Okay, so you're the bad cop. That means the good cop would be…let me go out on a limb here, Emily? Fine, go head, ask away, but understand I will not indulge any vulgar inquisitions into my private life." She hesitates and uses Sean's approach, "I'll give you three questions before I shut down. Choose wisely."

The women take a very loud sidebar.

"We have to know if they had sex," leads Emily.

Jen replies, "They had sex, for Christ's sake. She stayed over. Besides, didn't you observe him… He's now tall dark and not as edgy."

"Oh, for the love of God…we had sex. That is your one and only freebie. Let's go, clock is ticking. Laci, you're up…shoot."

"Hmm, so many missing details. Where does one start? Okay, like how frigging good was he on stage? Damn!"

Emily interjects before Maggie uses that as one of her questions, "I'm fast forwarding. Mags, one minute you were next to me, and the next you were gone, vanished. We get one text, 'w/ S Im fine.' What happened?"

Maggie takes them through her anxiety, the flirtatious tequila pour, the walk to the garden with Jim, the buildup, and the eventual performance on stage. "I felt manipulated in some way, and then I got pissed, like really pissed." She details the tension in his office and his quick exit, leaving Becca to watch over her. "He called me a flight risk!" They all arch their eyebrows at her. Next, she describes the photos in his office that simultaneously revealed so little and so much. It was his ability to apply reason to the situation that threw her. "And then he kissed me, so I said sneak me out the back and I'll go with you."

It's Jen's turn. "Okay, that places you at his house at about midnight, give or take... Was it like crash open the door and do it or what?"

Maggie gives an exasperated sigh. "That's question number 2, and no, it was nothing like that. Get a grip, girls, he had been working all day, and I had just totally lost it on him. He showered, I made him something to eat, we talked, had sex, slept, and I'm home."

Jen sits across from her. "You are full of shit. You're leaving something out."

"Look, Jen, it was a long, emotional conversation. I will tell you this much, he lost his mentor, brother, and mom by the time he was twenty-nine. The circumstances during and after which changed the course of his life. He's impressive, really."

Laci adds, "Impressive and hot for you, that's for sure."

Maggie gives her friend a quick grin of confirmation and informs them, "You have one question left."

The last question comes from Cassie, which she did not expect. "So you're about to have sex with someone you don't know very well. How awkward is it?"

Maggie looks at her friend and wants to be thoughtful knowing Cassie could be heading into a similar situation soon. "Well, everyone is different, but"—she pauses—"if you are thinking about awkwardness instead of having the kind of sex that ignites your soul, then the time and the man aren't right."

Danny pops his head in. "You aren't dressed? Move it, move it, move it, girls!"

CHAPTER 12

Put Me in Coach

Sean returns as the women are collecting towels, sneakers, and of course, champagne for their volleyball game. Laci is placing two champagne bottles in the thermos bag and lifts her head to ask, "How'd it go? Will Larry be allowed out to play this afternoon?"

"That I can neither confirm nor deny" is all Sean offers.

Maggie is in a chair with her back to him, Danny studying her intently. Sean is a little afraid for her to turn around, but when she does, Sean gives Danny a thumbs-up and says, "Looking badass, Maggie."

Danny replies, "I mean, was there really any other direction to take with this one?" While the other women are in bathing suits with a variety of patterns and colors, Maggie is in a black deep V-neck one-piece and LuLu Lemon leggings. Danny has masterfully applied a smoky eye and red lips and painted a tiny skull and cross bones on her left cheekbone with red glitter eyes. Sean takes in the other women. He was afraid they would all look like members of the line up at the Parrot on a Sunday night, but Danny has brought out each of their features in unique ways.

He freely compliments them, "Ladies, you look great. I don't know how well you'll play, but you're definitely going to turn heads when you walk in."

Jen gives a last call on mimosas as Danny shrieks, "No more alcohol. You've got two games to win." The women simultaneously flip him off. Jen gives him Laci's flamingo hat and a clipboard and whistle from Emily's car and starts singing, "Put me in coach, I'm ready to play…todaaay."

Upon shutting the trunk of Emily's car, Sean turns to Maggie and says, "You should ride with them. I'll catch up before you start playing."

"Oh, no, you don't. You wanted to hang with me today, that means getting to know this crew. Don't judge us 'cause we're ridiculous. We all have to return to reality on Monday, and that's gonna suck big-time." She puts on her helmet. He checks it and says, "Game time then."

The others pull out behind them, and Laci offers, "I wish her students could see her today."

Emily offers, "I'm glad her board can't."

Jen is staring out the window looking at her friend and says, "The person who really needs to see her today is Kevin. Seriously, dude, how could you let her go?"

Cassie adds, "Know what, I think it's all for the best…wherever it leads her."

Danny is riding shotgun and says, "I shouldn't have taken your alcohol away. You are way too serious!" With that, he hits the radio button, and "Uptown Funk" is blasting through the car, rallying his players.

As they park, Sean brings the helmets over to Emily and asks if he can toss them in. She is leaning into the cargo area with him and does a quick pulse check. "Give her space this afternoon, Sean, but don't leave her. She's got some issues." She struggles not to say too much and leaves her sentence unfinished.

Sean pulls out blankets and towels, places the helmets in the rear, turns to Emily, and says, "You can't get through life without issues, Emily. It's all part of the human condition."

Emily thinks to herself, *Please don't screw this up, Mags.*

Emily and Sean are a few feet behind the rest when Emily sees teams gathering. She turns to Sean and asks, "How's this go?"

"This time of year, we're lucky to get two teams out midseason. The competition ends around sunset. Last team standing gets free drinks at midnight, which is traditionally last call. Jesse will set the matches, and the rest is pretty standard stuff, four-man rotation. First team to twenty-one wins moves to next round."

"Got it. FYI, Cassie played at Penn State. We'll do okay."

"A ringer, nice. Good luck." As they exit the beach path, a few folks start making their way to Sean. He eyes Maggie standing next to Jen but is unable to follow the glare emanating from her blue eyes across the small gathering. Jesse approaches him with a clipboard. Sean makes a note, circles the starting teams, and heads over to greet a few regulars.

"Hey, Sean!" He turns to see a loyal customer coming toward him. "Amazing night last night at Darby's. So good to see you up there, man. Do it again soon, will ya?"

"Thanks, Bob, who you playing with?"

"Let's not get ridiculous, just here for the beer."

Sean looks out toward the ocean. The sun warms his back as he recalls looking down beach two days ago to see an unfamiliar figure in the distance, alone. What was she contemplating that day? He was drawn to the woman by the water but had no idea why. He continued to focus on her through the introductions to her friends. As he listened to their openness and warmth, he recognized a rare chemistry among women. But when she and Jen rejoined the group, her steel-blue eyes took him by surprise, challenging and assessing at the same time.

A whistle interrupts his thoughts, and he sees the players gather by Jesse to listen to the rules. Beyond the crowd is a woman in a black bathing suit and tutu who should be laughing with her friends instead of staring at the ocean again. He begins to wonder if he has unfairly interrupted her vacation with his own intentions. Simultaneously, his phone vibrates.

Yo...what r u looking for out there on the horizon.

He smiles. She has intentions too.

A mermaid.

She is playing volleyball. Ugh.

Do you know those women in the neon T's? If so, shut em down.

That's the plan...total bitches...bad blood.

Do I need to call for EMTs.

Very funny.

I heard you signed up to make dinner tonight for your friends.

Guilty.

We should do that.

We r going to, I just didn't tell you yet. Oops, GTG Game time.

Jen and Cassie return from the rules meeting and pull the girls into a huddle. "Seriously, what's with the neon Rehoboth 2014 shirts?" asks Cassie.

"I told you, no creativity. Newsflash, they will have tutus by tomorrow," remarks Jen as she eyes the other team.

Cassie is ready to give her pregame pep talk. "Someone needs to be the sub."

"I'll sub," volunteers Maggie. "Plus someone has to be ready to pop the champagne."

Cassie begins, "Laci, just get it over the net, but your primary role is distraction. Jen, let's set up a 2-2 diagonal. We need to make sure one of us is up front, one in the back. Emily, how's your serve?"

"Decent."

"Great, you lead off." Maggie has her head just above the huddle, a searing stare directed toward Heather. "Okay, Mags, just do that, like all game long. When we call sub, you're in. Tutus off on three."

Forty-five minutes later, they are holding their own, up 18–16.

"I can't take this much longer," Danny whines.

Maggie turns to him and says, "Call a time-out."

Sean is walking over toward them, and Maggie says, "Now, Danny, before Emily serves."

As the girls come toward Danny, he says, "Don't ask me... She wanted the time-out."

"Look, this is bullshit. I mean it's Heather. She sucks, Angie is a tramp, and the others are well vanilla ice cream, no toppings. We are the sprinkles on top of the ice cream, ladies! Cassie, you gotta believe in Laci and me, we can help. Jen, you need to coach from the side because you actually know what you are doing. And Laci, you and me, girl, batshit crazy on their asses. You ready?

"Matriarch, let's do this. I'm thirsty!"

Emily delivers the perfect serve, Laci and Maggie successfully return from the front, but as Angie short stuffs one to the middle of the front, Maggie steps left, and Cassie steps forward, leaps up, and spikes one dead center on them, 19–16.

Heather is serving for the opposition, out twice, 20–16.

Laci is serving. Maggie turns and whispers, "Hit it to that slut Angie. She can't take her eyes off Jesse." Laci executes as designed. Heather pushes Angie out of her way and gets it over the net, and Cassie steps up again to drop it right over the net, no coverage.

Whistle blows, Jesse points to the left side of the net smiling and says, "Victory, Femme Fatales."

Jen runs out. They are high fiving Cassie and cheering. Maggie runs and grabs a bottle of champagne as the girls start dragging Cassie to the ocean. Maggie runs to catch up, doubles back, and calls out, "Yo, Jessie!"

"Yeah, Maggie?"

"We forfeit the next round! This is victory enough!"

Danny turns to Sean and says, "What are they doing?"

"No idea, Danny, just enjoying the view."

As the women hit the water's edge, they are jumping and waving Maggie toward them. Maggie is shaking the champagne, unwrapping the bottleneck as she nears them, and pops the cork as the water hits her feet, spraying her friends as they grab the bottle and drink what they can. Laci and Maggie push the other three until they are knee-deep, kicking and splashing as the others squeal. Emily, Jen, and Cassie make the move to head out of the water, and Sean bends to grab towels. He shoves three at Danny and says, "Let's go."

Danny snidely remarks, "I guess chivalry is not dead."

As they head to the women, Sean once again is laser focused on the water. He hears, "Oh my god, thanks, Sean," and answers, "No problem."

Emily adds, "She may swim to Ireland, Sean. I wouldn't wait for her." She gets no response. She, Jen, and Cassie huddle together to head up beach, and Emily says, "Someone stick a fork in him."

Laci and Maggie are holding hands running deeper into the water, laughing. Laci turns to Maggie, pauses, and runs, shivering back toward Danny. Maggie eyes a cresting wave, and before it breaks, she dives, only to emerge just past the white caps, arms raised and shaking her hair. She dives under another wave before walking toward him without as much as a shiver.

Sean has his arms around Maggie, attempting to block some of the wind on the beach. She stops midway toward her friends, and as he turns to ask what is wrong, she takes her wet towel, flips it over his neck, pulling him toward her, and kisses him. "No more searching for mermaids, got it?"

"Don't need to. Caught one."

Maggie and Sean are the last of their group to exit. Maggie has pulled off her leggings and put on her Patagonia quarter zip and boyfriend jeans. She waves to Jesse and interlocks her arm with Sean's as they hit the street, making their way to Emily's SUV. The tailgate is up, wet clothes and towels on the asphalt.

As they catch up with her friends, Maggie and the others hear the tail end of a comment from Heather's minivan in the next row of parking spaces, "I guess she is having her revenge, but has the ink even dried on her divorce from Kevin yet?"

Jen and Cassie's eyes widen. Emily cautions, "Easy, Mags, not worth it." Laci hands Maggie a motorcycle helmet and says, "Bullshit, let her have it."

Maggie throws down her damp towel and marches over to Heather, whose friends have left her standing alone to face the impending wrath as they murmur and snicker like a pack of high school girls.

Maggie's stride and facial expression are like a Chester County thunderstorm that hits with force and fury at the end of a humid summer day. "Listen here, you passive-aggressive bitch, don't talk about things you don't understand. Kevin and I are divorced, so if that beautiful man and I want to shag till the cows come home, it's none of your goddamn business." The parking lot is now silent.

"And in the future, whether you see me at Wegman's or some lame-ass Christmas party, head in the other direction because,

Heather, these are the last three words you'll ever hear from me…
Go fuck yourself!"

As Maggie turns to head toward the bike, Jen says to Sean, "She's
really kind of eloquent, don't you think?" Emily studies Sean, trying
to determine the look in his eyes: pride, amusement…oh no, much
more than that. The proverbial fork is in, and she fears it is in deep.

Sean picks up his helmet, meets her at the bike, and says, "You
don't really strike me as the lame-ass Christmas-party type."

She gives him half a smile. "Take me back to my house, Sean?
I need a shower."

CHAPTER 13

Dance Lessons

After dropping by Sean's house to exercise Rosie in the backyard and trade the Harley for the Jeep, they head for the rental. Maggie's phone rings to the sound of Grace Potter singing "Hot Summer Nights" as she opens the back door and waves Sean in. "Hey, kiddo, what's up?"

Maggie walks away from Sean, using steady reassuring words to the caller. She looks at Sean and mouths, "Sorry," but he softly says, "All good."

The girls pile into the house, and Jen asks, "Who she on the phone with, kids or work?"

Maggie gives Jen the hush-up sign as she tries to end the call. "Yes, that's Jen. No, no, you are not talking to her right now… She's drunk. Okay, have a great time tonight. We will talk when I get home. Love you."

"Seriously, Mags, you have to tell your mini-me I'm too drunk to talk at four in the afternoon? You know she idolizes me. She okay?"

"Oh yeah, total hero worship, she's fine. Usual stuff."

Jen turns to Sean. "Maggie's middle child gives her a run for her money in sooo many ways." Jen's phone vibrates. She laughs. "Ha! Busted, Maggie Burke." She continues to read, "'Why is my mom being shady?'"

"Oh, puhleeze… I'm taking a shower. Can someone figure out how many for dinner by the time I get out?"

Dressed in jeans, an ivory embroidered peasant blouse, and silver jewelry, Maggie heads to the kitchen but not before glancing outside to see her friends entertaining Sean. *God help me*, she thinks as she moves toward the fridge to pull out assorted vegetables, butter, and herbs. She pulls a wrapped apron out of one of her reusable grocery bags and places it on the dining table as well as select ingredients from home, brown sugar, fresh garlic, spices, a fresh jar of Dijon, Worcestershire sauce, olive oil, and balsamic vinegar.

Laci pops her head in the slider. "Mags, we invited Larry and Scott, and they're coming over...that makes nine. Sean wants to know if we need more fish."

"We're good."

"All right then, we're just gonna keep him busy out here, out of your way...okay?"

"Yeah, fine... Tunes please."

Laci shuts the door, turns, and says, "All right, she's in her happy place. Jen, you're on tunes... Let's open some wine and dish."

The women rotate in and out for showers, checking to see if Maggie needs help while filling Sean in on the significance of their annual trip and some of their antics. An hour and a half later, the door opens again, but this time it's Maggie stepping onto the deck to bring out grilled asparagus wrapped in prosciutto and an olive tapenade crostini. Scott and Sean are out of their seats to help her with trays as she remarks, "Oh my gosh, it's freezing out here. Come inside. Scott, Larry, no one told me you had gotten here. Welcome!"

The dining table has been fully set with candles, wineglasses, and a variety of wine. Scott walks toward the kitchen, handing Maggie a bouquet of flowers. "Maggie, what smells so good?"

"That's Jen's baked brie. It's heaven and just about ready."

"Be right over, Mags, pouring you a glass... Pick your poison."

"Pinot noir, please. And, Mr. DeMarco, just because you are not in your restaurant does not mean you have the night off. I have a job for you."

Scott delivers Maggie's wine and says, "That's it, Maggie, put him to work. The man suffers from a serious lack of direction. He didn't even bring you your wine, tsk, tsk."

Maggie's eyes twinkle in Scott's direction as she pulls Sean toward the sink, where she explains what temperature she would like the outdoor grill and what she put into the rub for the salmon. She gently lays the two full sides of salmon skin down on the presoaked cedar planks, leaving Sean to finish the prep. Two aluminum pans of sliced potatoes and onions are roasting in the oven, and a large wooden bowl filled with Boston lettuce, radicchio, endive, dried cherries, and candied pecans is waiting to be dressed.

Maggie takes an empty glass honey jar and begins concocting her homemade dressing. Both Sean and Scott are studying her closely as she works in ingredients, measuring by sight only. She turns around and says, "You can both stop trying to figure out my recipe, you won't be able to duplicate it…and if you try, I may have to kill you."

Sean heads to the grill, Scott in tow, and Cassie comes over to help by slicing the ciabatta for two baskets, placing them in the table with the seasoned dipping oil, red pepper flakes, and grated cheese, per Maggie's instruction.

Maggie quickly places name cards made from champagne corks and sharpies at each place setting, spreading out the men and strategically placing Sean between Laci and Cassie. Platters of fish, potatoes, and the salad bowl join the bouquet of flowers to complete the table scape as Maggie asks everyone if they are hungry.

Conversation is communal and easy as if they all had been friends for years. Maggie is about to clear the dishes, and Em places a hand on her wrist. "First of all, you are not doing the dishes, and secondly, I don't think you heard Larry's question. Please repeat it, Larry."

"Maggie, if you had to say, who would you think is the best dancer here tonight?"

Maggie looks at Em and whispers, "Did I miss something?" She smiles encouragingly, and Maggie answers, "Well, given the pending performance tomorrow night, I would say Laci and Danny." Danny hops up, heads toward her, and gives her a kiss on her cheek. Larry pouts.

"Larry's jealous because I found you girls first."

Scott clears his throat from the far end of the table, looking directly at Sean, and says, "Actually, that's not correct. Someone here has taken several years of instruction."

Maggie responds, "It was Irish dancing, and I was a child."

"Interesting, very interesting, don't you think, Sean? Better tell her before I do."

Maggie gives him a quizzical look as Sean explains, "I was kind of a tough kid, and after Tony left for college, there was no one to help my mother keep me in line. So when I was caught selling cigarettes in the bathroom at school and got expelled—"

Maggie interrupts, "Cigarettes, Sean, really? That got you expelled?"

He is now smirking. "Let's say a variety of cigarettes, yes. Anyway, my mother was beside herself. She transferred me to Catholic school and asked the nuns to show me some discipline. Their answer was to sign me and other problem kids up for ballroom dance classes."

Maggie looks at Emily, who is starting to giggle, Jen, who is already in full belly laugh, and Cassie, who is howling. As it sinks in, Maggie's mind goes to the photo of the little boy with the bad attitude, and she begins to laugh, loud and hard, just as Laci adds, "Too bad they hadn't invented my favorite move yet, Sean... I'd love to see those nuns doing the Jersey turnpike with each other." With that, the table erupts, and there is not a dry eye in the house.

As those that did not cook clean the kitchen, Maggie, Jen, Sean, and Scott adjourn to the great room. Upon Jen's request, Sean and Scott fill her in on Jim's life, including his wife, Eileen, and her battle with breast cancer.

"It came back about twelve years ago. Jim was still teaching at Wharton, but Eileen had long retired from nursing after the first round. I don't know who it was harder on, do you, Scott?"

"Him...definitely him. She was a fighter. That brogue would come out the angrier she got, and she was very angry about all they put her through." Scott imitates Eileen's brogue, "I'm little more than a wee lab rat to them."

"Wait a minute... Eileen was from Ireland? He told me he left a girl in Ireland at the end of WWII."

Sean explains, "He did. He came back to Philadelphia, wrote to her every day, and mailed them once a week. She never replied. He enrolled at Penn on the GI Bill and immersed himself in economics."

Scott picks up the story, "But she, too, was busy over on the Emerald Isle. She studied her ass off and applied to Penn's Nursing School…got in two years later. She never let him know she was coming to America."

Scott finishes, "Jim thought he was making a complete fool of himself and moping his way down Locust Walk one day, and who does he see, Eileen heading toward the dining hall in her nursing uniform and navy cape. He had her on a date by Friday night, married six months later."

Maggie adds, "That little devil." Jen is near tears, and Sean lightens the mood. "Scott, remember when Jim asked his colleague for marijuana from the research labs at the hospital?"

"Oh my, I had forgotten about that," Scott replies as he starts to laugh. Sean continues, "They asked me to come over and teach them how to smoke it. So I called Scott for backup. They were well into their seventies, and I was a little nervous, but she was having a terrible time keeping anything down."

Maggie flippantly asks, "Sean, are you a stoner?"

"Maggie, I went to Drexel in the late seventies, I practically majored in it. I outgrew it. Anyway, Jim's colleague had given him a vile full of ready-to-use laboratory-grown pot. I rolled one joint, licked it, lit it, and took a hit… It was potent. I handed it over to Jim and Eileen, and they were inhaling as if someone had handed them back their Chesterfields.

"Twenty minutes later, they were a couple of giggling teenagers and raiding the kitchen. Scott and I hung out but tried to stay out of their way. When they took it upstairs, we cleaned up the cookie batter and Doritos and had ourselves a good laugh. The next day, Jim was…shall we say, a little happier, and I showed him how to roll half joints in order to not overdo it with her.

"It helped her through the worst of it, but Jim stoned…that is a memory I shall cherish forever." Maggie and Jen were smiling, each thinking about their parents stoned on medical marijuana.

Scott and Larry offer to take Danny home as Maggie heads back to her room to pull a few things together. Jen follows and shuts the door. "Mags, he's great."

"Jen, please don't. I'm moving through this, but I'm hanging by a thread here. I mean, he is great, but he's here, and in thirty-six hours, I won't be. What am I doing to myself?"

"Geez, Maggie, it's an hour and half from home. You'd drive longer than that to see the Eagles play on Sunday, and you know it!"

"It's two hours, he owns a restaurant, works weekends, and I work six days a week, fifty-two weeks a year. It can't work, it won't work."

"Listen to me. You have thirty-six hours left. Open the vault, Maggie, at least a little. He wants to know more about you, but we wouldn't go there. If you open yourself up a little, maybe you'll find it would be worth figuring out."

"He was asking you questions about me? Is he serious with that shit? Should I pull my résumé out to fill in any blanks before we go at it tonight?" Maggie's temper was starting to rise.

"Oh, for crying out loud, Maggie, did you listen to me?"

"I did." Maggie almost puts her bag back on her bed. However, as annoyed as she may be, the truth of the matter is, she wants one more night. She will never be here again, and as much as that is starting to weigh heavily on her, she knows she has unfinished business with the stud in the great room. She tosses the overnight bag over her shoulder, grabs her cape, and struts toward the said stud with a smile on her face and a sparkle in her eyes.

CHAPTER 14

Take the Long Way Home

Maggie is waiting by the Jeep. "Do you want me to drive? How much wine did your dinner partners ply into you?"

"I feel okay, but I'm probably over the limit, so yeah, that works." Sean walks her to the driver's side and presses her up against the Jeep. "Now, Maggie, this is not your Audi. The transmission does not shift easily, so don't let the clutch out too fast. You have to be patient and deliberate with it."

He kisses her deliberately but not patiently, which she thoroughly enjoys before saying, "Kiss me like that again, Sean, and we won't get out of the driveway."

Maggie handles the Jeep like a pro, zipping along Boardwalk Avenue, windows down enough to let the sea air in and listening to Sean recap the evening. He remarks on the natural balance between the women, siting both similarities and distinctions between them all. He turns to Maggie and says, "Do you entertain a lot, Maggie? Tonight looked effortless for you."

"I used to. I love doing it. Matching the food with the wine, the seating, the table setting…it all should coordinate."

"It took me a long time to figure that out for Darby's. It still needs work."

Maggie slows as they approach the center of town, moving slowly by the hotels. It has been a beautiful Veteran's Day weekend, and the hotels are crowded. As she waits for people to cross the street, Sean turns to her and asks, "Would you like to get some ice cream?

There's a great place about three blocks from here, down on the right."

Maggie smiles to herself, charmed by the boy inside this man. "Are you asking me out on a date, Sean?" she teases.

"I believe I am. What do you say?"

"What the heck, why not?"

"Still not a simple yes, but again, I'll take it."

As they wait in line for their turn at the window, Maggie studies him closely. He is relaxed in a way that she suspects he has not experienced in some time. She credits her friends and a full day away from work, but she also credits herself. She is having a palpable effect on him. He smiles just past her. Maggie turns to see the object of his amusement to find a six-year-old little girl staring up at her.

Maggie quickly connects; this is one of the little girls she gave her glow sticks to at the bonfire. Round eyes gaze at Maggie with a hint of fear. Maggie crouches to be at eye level with this pint-sized darling. "Hi, Lily. Your name is Lily, right?" She gets a nod of confirmation, so Maggie continues. "And your sister is Stella."

Lily smiles, "And you are Ms. Maggie. Are you getting ice cream because we are too! But the line is sooo long."

"Well, you can wait with us. Where's your Mom, Lily?"

By the time Maggie has heard the very detailed story of why Lily is not standing with her mother, she hears a woman calling out Lily's name with a touch of panic in her voice. Sean raises his hand and waves, "We've got her."

Lily's mother approaches with her older sister in tow, "Sean? Wow, you are out on a Saturday night?" She observes Maggie with obvious curiosity as she continues, "I can't believe you recognized her, thanks." She focuses in a new direction, "Hi, are you, Maggie? My girls can't stop talking about you. I bet Lily saw your cape. She thinks you look like Snow White in it."

Sean begins to fill in the blanks for Maggie, telling her that Lily and Stella are actually Jesse's nieces. He watches as Maggie listens without ever taking her attention from Lily. They are deep in conversation about the pitfalls of being a younger sister, when it becomes their turn to order. As Sean offers to fill mother and daughters' orders, Lily whines, "Do I have to order vanilla, Mom?"

Maggie smiles at the young mother before telling Lily, "I'm getting vanilla. It's the very best ice cream to have with rainbow sprinkles!"

Stella has now joined in, "Me too. I want vanilla with rainbow sprinkles."

A lecture from her big sister to Lily about not dropping her cone threatens tears. Maggie quickly intervenes. She removes the pink-and-gray Chan Lu wrap bracelet from her wrist and wraps it around Lily's. "Here, this is one of my lucky bracelets. It's time for me to pass its magic on to someone else. Wear it, and you will never drop your ice cream again." She then reaches into her bag to pull out a small plastic bag of cheap makeup from Walmart and turns to Stella, "And this is for you because you are much older, but you should only use it for dress up."

Sean hands out cones, including his very adult bourbon pecan and her juvenile vanilla with rainbow sprinkles. Maggie suggests a walk, and as Sean takes her hand, he asks, "Who are you, Mary Poppins? Those girls are usually a handful."

"I don't know, Sean. I just get kids. Was one, had some. It's just easy for me."

She looks into his eyes and sees something not clicking with him. Before he can become awkward, she turns the conversation back to his comfort zone and asks what business associations exist in Rehoboth. He talks about the Chamber of Commerce and describes the nuances of living in a growing beach community striving to maintain its small-town identity. She listens intently, thinking how difficult it would be to run his business amid the ebb and flow of a seasonal crowd of vacationers. Yet she feels his restaurant is a mainstay in the town, which means he is as well. She considers him determining; big fish, little pond.

Suddenly, they are across from Darby's, and he stops. She exclaims, "No, no, no! You are not going in there in the middle of a date with me."

He swings her around and kisses her. "I would never think of it. I just never look at it from over here."

"You should. It needs a little emphasis on the front door, you know, enhance the curb appeal a bit. It would not take much. The outside entrance does not match the ambiance inside, which is so welcoming as soon as you open the door. I felt it right away the other night."

"You mean last night."

"Whoa, does that freak you out a little too?"

"Not freaked, more amazed actually." He uses the opportunity to push her a little as they continue to walk. He recalls Emily's advice to start where Maggie is comfortable. "Tell me about your kids, Maggie."

She surrenders and opens the vault, just a crack. "Let's turn around, and I'll try to finish this up by the time we get to the car.

"Caroline is my oldest, a stunningly beautiful woman, although she doesn't see it. She awards trust slowly, but once earned, she is intensely loyal. She has high moral standards but does not impose them on others. She is one of my best friends, dependable, and genuinely concerned about both of her parents. But my favorite thing about her is that we share the same sense of humor and can be a bit devilish together."

Maggie opens her phone, accesses her photos, and selects one of Caroline. She hands the phone to Sean. "Look past the obvious beauty and take in the warmth of her smile, that's Caroline."

Sean responds, "She must have given you a lot to worry about when she was younger."

"Not a single worry, Sean. She and I worked through some mother-daughter stuff with a great therapist in her early teens, and it provided the foundation for the friendship we have today. We are two open books with each other." She flips to another photo as they wait to cross the street.

Sean looks at a young athletic woman, maybe twenty-five, with hazel eyes, long, dark wavy hair pulled into a ponytail coming out of an Eagles baseball cap, and a bridge of freckles across her nose. She is staring intently as the photographer took the photo, crouched by her dog as she gazes toward a lake. "This is Lindsey, my second child." Sean notes that Maggie does not use the term middle child, and for some reason he is impressed with that.

"Jen called her my mini-me not because of her looks but because of her attitude. Poor kid got the best and worst of my personality traits. I worked hard with her to teach her how to control her temper, because contrary to what anyone may think, I do not relish mine. In a word, she is intense. Linds feels things acutely, leads with passion, and accepts defeat poorly. She is a sharp thinker, a problem solver. When she was younger, she lived to make her sister laugh, and at holidays when they are back under my roof, I can hear them laughing together in their childhood room, and it fills my heart with joy."

"She's all you, Maggie, a natural beauty. I know the coloring is different, but look at the set of her jaw, the intensity of her gaze. She's the Grace Potter fan, right?"

"She is, and Bob Dylan. At least I did something right with that kid."

They've reached the Jeep, and Sean offers, "I think the ice cream and the walk cleared my head. How about I drive and you can tell me about your son." By the time he has settled in his seat, Maggie has pulled up a photo of Patrick taken on campus in October when she went up to visit him at Tufts.

Maggie studies the photo as Sean begins to drive. "It's so much harder to look at your boy and see a man than it is to see your girls as women. I have no idea why. Maybe because he's my youngest."

She continues by asking a rhetorical question, "Did you ever know someone who was inherently good? Patrick does not see the bad in anyone, ever. He refuses to pass judgment or blame. He stands by his decisions. He moves through life with optimism and a sense of wonder that I envy. In addition, he loves with abandon, which scares the hell out of me. I worry about him because of all my children, he is the one who will be judged, blamed, criticized, and taken advantage of, not because he is gay, because he is good. And that is rare in today's world."

Sean pulls into his driveway and gently takes her phone to look at the photo. "But he has you, his sisters, and I assume his father.

That's a lot, Maggie. He'll be okay." He hands it back to her thinking her son is the child that most clearly resembles her.

"So those are my children. Now, why did you ask?"

"Because I've seen you through only one lens, mine. After spending today with you and your friends, I started to see you through some other ones. The fact that you didn't talk about your children's accomplishments or GPAs shows me what kind of lens you see your children and they you."

"Damn it, Sean, you're killing me. I'm trying so hard not to let you wear me down, to ignore the fact that tomorrow is the last time I will probably see you, and then you do this, you blow me away with your depth and leave me wanting more time. Which is something I cannot have."

He steps out of the Jeep, manually opens his garage door, hops back in, and says, "Draw no conclusions, Maggie, because honestly when you do, you're killing me too. We have to ignore the time factor in all this."

"I'll try…but… Sean?"

"Yes?"

She smiles at him and says, "You really can't afford an automatic garage door?" He produces a rare smile in response, and she mentally notes that this sort of ribbing is a rarity in his life. The knowledge of which makes her a little sad, and she catches herself because she suspects he would hate that reaction. Still, not such a tight ass after all.

Maggie calls for Rosie as she enters the house through the garage door, knowing the poor dog expects to see her from the front porch. Rosie barrels through the house and jumps on the couch before seeing Maggie and Sean enter the anterior room through the laundry room.

Sean chastises, "Rosie, get down! And, Maggie, stop encouraging her to act like a maniac."

Maggie is on the couch with Rosie, giving her an all-over rubdown. "Sean, this house is gorgeous, but it's extremely orderly. You need a little chaos. It's good for your soul."

Sean has picked up a remote control and punched in a code that fills the lower level with music. Maggie is looking at the fireplace, set among deep-set bookshelves, when she sees something of interest. "Sean, what's in that leather case?"

He reaches for it and places it on the coffee table. He begins to build a fire. "It's an antique board game set. Open it."

Maggie opens the set to find checkers, dice, backgammon discs, and hand-carved chess pieces. She picks up the onyx queen, studying its artistry as he continues.

"After Edwin passed, I spent more and more time here, trying to hold on to as much of my brother as I could. Board games were something Edwin loved, and Tony had no choice but to love them too. So when I would visit, we would play. At first, it was chess, when he became too tired to concentrate on that it was backgammon, and eventually checkers. But the conversations were always more important than the victory."

"I get it. Having something to concentrate on occupies your mind, alleviating the stress of the situation. And you have to be creative so your mood is elevated."

"Would you be willing to take this to the front porch? I can drop the side blinds to buffer the wind, and there is a table and chairs that would save our backs tomorrow."

Maggie grabs the mohair blanket as Sean closes the fireplace doors. She looks at the neatly stacked wood and thinks she will never see that fire lit. She fights the growing anxiety tightening in her chest and, as he picks up the leather case, turns and recognizes it immediately.

"Three harmless questions."

She smiles at the familiarity of his request. "Okay, shoot."

"Standards or tenors?"

"Tenors, at least to start."

Sean punches something into the remote, and Andrea Bocelli begins. "Port or brandy?"

"Port." She is now smiling at the calming effect of the benign questions.

They stop at the dry bar in the living room, and Sean pulls a bottle from the back and hands it to her as he retrieves the appropriate glassware. "Jim considers this his private stock, but I'm sure he'd be willing to share. He's sort of smitten with you."

Maggie opens the front door and wraps the blanket around herself as Sean pulls the side blinds and flips an outdoor switch that illuminates the heating units on the ceiling of the front porch. Maggie allows a gasp of delight to escape as she exclaims, "Oh, I think I love this feature," as she feels a wave of warmth come over her.

Sean plugs in the strung Edison lights and teases her, "Really, the heating panels, not the sound system? I'm a little disappointed." He pulls a chair out for Maggie at the game table. "Okay, question three, backgammon or chess?"

Maggie takes the leather game case from him, places it on the table, and pulls him to her. "The sound system is awesome, but I expected as much. Okay, mister, my game of choice is backgammon because my head is not clear enough for chess tonight. Just don't think you're going to be unchallenged. I played a lot of this in college."

They are two games in, narrow victories for each of them. The conversation is lighthearted, talking about strong likes and dislikes. They find they are both democrats, not a surprise. Sean reveals that he chose Rottweilers because he liked their aloofness and confidence, and Maggie talks about the ever-social Labrador traits and fondness for rescue dogs.

As they talk about college and first careers, Maggie muses that they may have walked past each other in Philadelphia dozens of times and never known it. The dice are starting to roll Maggie's way, and she is relaxed, thinking she may as well reopen the vault. She keeps her focus on the board and asks, "Do you think we all have defining moments from our youth that shape how we move through life?"

As she moves her game pieces, Sean responds, "Not necessarily. I think we have to stay open to having lots of them throughout our lives. One of my defining moments came in 1984, but there have been others. And I think other people stay closed off so they never have them."

He rolls, advancing three pieces to the next board. "How about you, Maggie? I'm sure holding your newborns was one."

"Oh yeah, the best moments for sure. But there have been some tough ones too." She pauses and looks into his eyes. He refuses to fill the void for her, but not in any kind of demeaning way. She sees only patience. Maggie thinks to herself, *Another layer to this man. Good grief, I am so screwed.*

She inhales deeply and says, "Remember how emotional I got last night when you told me about losing the people you loved?" Sean nods reassuringly. "Well, Patrick is only part of the reason I got so upset. I had a brother who was killed in Vietnam in 1970."

Maggie unfolds the story of her oldest brother, Patrick. Her brother had been drafted into the Army, served in the Fourth Infantry Division and deployed before she began second grade. "I was a little girl. All I knew was that my father was proud, my mother worried, and my older sister and brothers were angry. They listed his name in the church bulletin each week with other boys requesting prayers of peace and protection for our parish soldiers.

"My oldest sister, Kate, was a senior in high school and applying to non-Catholic universities, which pretty much had my dad at his wit's end. She had begun to get involved in antiwar demonstrations, which caused a lot of friction in our house. My brothers were furious with her, my father ignored her arguments, and my mother said the rosary. Our house was a hotbed of tension on any given day.

"Well, the school year ended, and Kate was heading off to Penn State in the fall. One Sunday morning in mid-July as we were all getting ready for Mass, a group of men came to our door, some in Army uniforms, the police chief, and our family doctor. They came to tell my parents the news that their son had been killed in action and that his remains would be coming into Dover Air Force base on Wednesday."

She looks lost in the memory before continuing, "It was like a giant vortex had swept in and sucked the life out of us. My dad closed the Tavern and busied himself with preparations for the Mass with members of his VFW club. My mother did not get out of bed for three days. I remember Kate telling my dad that my mother needed the pills the doctor had left, but my father refused to give them to her.

"Somehow, we all survived to Friday, the day of the funeral. My older sisters made sure my five-year-old sister and I were in clean summer dresses and sandals for Mass. My dad must have given my mom something because she was dressed and ready to go.

"My uncle Tommy, an Augustinian priest at Villanova, agreed to say the Mass and arranged for a choir of IHM nuns to sing." She pauses and then offers a weak smile. "I still don't think I've ever seen so many nuns in one place."

Maggie is starring at the board as she continues, "When we arrived at St. Coleman's, there were protestors lining the sidewalk. I read their signs and felt my chest tighten. My brother Jimmy hugged me to keep me from crying. My father was enraged. He told us to stay in the car, but Kate would not have it. Before he reached the protestors, she was beside him and took his hand. She said something to the protestors, held up her hand with the peace sign, and all the signs were dropped."

Maggie's eyes clouded with the memory look through him. "Kate waved at us to get out of the limo and walked back to us with her arm around my dad. We lined up outside of church, behind the coffin draped in the American flag, Kate with my dad, Jimmy and Jack flanking my mother, and the three youngest girls falling in behind. The church was packed, and I remember feeling like I was going to lose my parents in the crowd.

"I was so young, Sean, I didn't understand it all. I had just made Holy Communion in May. Pat had sent a letter written just for me. That made me feel so special to get my own letter from him." Maggie's eyes are now welling with tears. "I thought my brother was a hero. Why was everyone so sad when he was so brave?" She tries hard to swallow the lump in her throat. "Somewhere in the middle of Mass, I decided it was because he wasn't in heaven yet."

A teardrop escapes down her cheek as she continues, "It was time for Communion, and the O'Rourke family exited our pew to receive the Eucharist. Do you remember in 1970, we all had just started taking the Eucharist in our hands?"

She resumes without an answer, "And as I stood in front of my uncle to receive, I took the host and turned to my left instead of my right, slid between people in line, up to the top of the casket, got on my toes, and placed the host on one of the stars on the flag. Before I knew it, my first-grade teacher, Sr. Anne, gently put her arm around me and led me to the vestibule. When she asked me if I was okay, I simply said, 'Yes, but I think Jesus should be with Pat right now.'" Tears freely steam from her eyes now.

"Sr. Anne somehow managed to slide me back in the pew with my family. My brother Jack placed me on his lap and told me to be a good girl, we were almost done. He had no idea where I had been. The procession and burial only further confused me.

"My dad stayed behind as my brothers and sisters put my mother in the limousine clutching Patrick's flag as the bagpipes played 'Danny Boy.' Marty O'Rourke greeted each mourner as they came up to place flowers on Pat's casket. I watched him from under a tree. After everyone had gone, my dad genuflected by the casket and wept. I went over to him, and he hugged me and said, "I was very proud of you for sharing your Communion with your brother, Maggie. Look, it's gone, Patty took it to heaven with him."

She lifts her eyes to Sean. He meets hers with warmth and compassion, as she concludes, "My dad kept me by his side as the reception at the Tavern carried on. That day, my father taught me that life has to go on in spite of the circumstances we are handed. He allowed my mother time, but after three months, they had the one and only fight I can recall. He threw out the pills, yelling at her to care for the six children she still had left. After that, my dad closed the bar on Sundays to spend the day with his family. In time, my mother also accepted that life goes on."

Maggie mechanically picks up the game pieces, packing them away, and Sean takes her hand, stands, and pulls her to him. While in his embrace, she wonders if her raw emotion will be too much for him. She looks up to meet his eyes and says, "Kevin once told me I was void of any emotion beyond anger. I've only ever told that story to one other person…my therapist. It took me over a year and eight thousand dollars to do it. I found out I have a plethora of emotions, and that is why we are not married anymore. Why do I feel you could have pulled this out of me if we had met earlier? Where were you when I needed you, Sean?"

"I'm here now, Maggie, I'm right here." His hand has not broken its hold on hers, and he lifts it to his heart. "I know exactly what you mean."

An alert sounds on Sean's phone, breaking the moment. He checks to see a weather alert for a nor'easter heading their way by late Sunday morning. He shows Maggie the alert. "Here we go. You now get to experience the downside of living at the beach. I could use your help pulling a few things in out here and checking over at Jim's."

Sean calls Becca instructing her to get the staff to put the sandbags by all doors as part of lockup. Then he and Maggie tie up the blinds, disconnect the Edison lights, remove the bulbs, cover outlets, and lock in the heating units before they take furniture to the garage.

Jim's porch has a single chair out. Sean quietly unlocks the front door and places it inside as Maggie keeps an eye on the stairs for Jim. They shut the door lock it and scurry back. Rosie is waiting for them on the landing as they reenter the house. Maggie lets out a yawn as they place glasses in the dishwasher and grab water before going to bed.

Sean hands her the small duffel bag and says, "Go on upstairs and get into bed. I'll be up in a minute." She gives him a sleepy kiss and does as he requests. He warmly considers this worn-out Maggie, thinking it is probably a rarity.

Once upstairs, Maggie barely washes her face and teeth, strips, and grabs the flannel shirt off the back of the door before sliding into bed. Sean enters the bedroom a few minutes later to find a head full of curls falling against his pillow. As he readies for bed, he hears Rosie jump onto the bed, again nothing from Maggie. He gives Rosie a cookie and slides her to the foot of the bed. As he gets in, Maggie reaches for him and nuzzles in. She whispers, "You never told me your birthday."

"March seventeenth," he replies and watches a grin come across her face before she falls soundly asleep.

CHAPTER 15

Lifelines

Maggie hears an alarm and feels movement in the bed. The wind has picked up outside. Rosie is curled by her feet. Sean checks his phone in the darkness. He turns his head, kisses her forehead as he silences the alarm, sits up, and says, "Good morning. Don't get up, go back to sleep."

Maggie rolls onto her back, stretches, gives Sean a confused look, and asks, "Why in the world are you awake?"

He reaches to turn on the light on his nightstand. "I have to go someplace. I'll be back by nine thirty, ten at the latest."

She is up like a shot. "What? Seriously, where are you going?"

He recalls Emily's advice again, "Just don't leave her," and starts over. "Okay, I should have mentioned this earlier, but it's been a little hectic, don't you think?"

"That depends…where are you going?" Eyes no longer clouded by sleep or exhaustion, she focuses in on him with precision. He suspects she could be in full storm mode within minutes, so he calmly continues.

Sean walks her through his Sunday ritual. He rises, tends to Rosie, showers, and heads to the shelter to help make Sunday breakfast, citing that Saturday night is the highest guest count each week. The weather has turned colder, and in light of the storm that seems to have arrived early, he knows it will be a larger crowd, possibly a hundred.

"I want to help."

"It can be kind of rough, Maggie."

"Oh my god, are you serious with that? I run a nonprofit. I have been in shelters. I get it. I want the shower first. Put Rosie out, give her breakfast, and by then the bathroom will be all yours."

Sean smiles. "You're very bossy, you know that?"

"I think you need it, Sean." The flannel shirt is tossed off two steps before opening the bathroom door, and as Sean announces to Rosie it's time to go out, he realizes there is a missed opportunity in that shower.

Maggie has on a black quarter zip, her jeans from last night, and sneakers. She heads downstairs as Sean showers, looks for rain gear, spots it in the laundry room, and grabs an obnoxious yellow jacket. She looks in the mirror by the coat hooks and applies her essentials, powder, blush, gloss, mascara. Satisfied, she tosses her makeup bag on top of the dryer and calls up to Sean as she pulls her hair into a ponytail. "Hurry up! We're gonna be—" Sean has opened the door from the garage, smiling. "Late."

The shelter is located a block behind the outlets just off the Coastal Highway. There is no street sign announcing the building as they pull into the parking lot. Maggie squints through the pouring rain and sees something above the doorway. Sean pulls up to the front door, and Maggie has the door open before he can move. "Just wait right inside the door for me. I have to get you signed in. Did you bring your license?"

"All set."

As Sean pulls away Maggie looks up at the sign, the Tony DeMarco Home for Men. She loves that it does not say shelter. She steps inside and takes off her jacket to let it drip on the entrance rug while she takes in her surroundings. The front desk looks like a hotel desk from the fifties, and the entire lobby looks like midcentury Miami. A nun in a light-blue habit walks toward her, and Maggie wonders who wears habits anymore. Before the nun can reach her, Sean opens the door, taking his jacket off as well.

The nun appears to be over seventy-five and has fixed her attention on Sean as she says, "Am I glad to see you! We'll be busy today. Seventy-two stayed last night, and no one is in a hurry to go back out in this mess."

Sean introduces Maggie to Sr. Jeanne, who promptly hustles them toward the chapel for Mass. *Somehow I missed the memo on Mass*, wonders Maggie, *but when in Rome.* The entrance to the chapel is a pale-pink archway with a dedication plaque that reads Mary DeMarco Chapel. Sean slips her into the last pew of the tiny chapel and whispers, "Get ready for the fastest Mass you'll ever attend."

There is no priest, a nun stands to deliver the first and second readings, and a deacon reads the gospel, no homily. Sr. Jeanne and the nun from the readings stand by the deacon during consecration. Men begin to enter the chapel. Most get in line for communion, even though they missed the readings. Sean once again fills in the blanks, "We go last."

Maggie watches as the men file in, counting at least fifty in a line wrapped around the pews. Suddenly Maggie sees Danny in line and looks at Sean, who seems to be unfazed. Sean steps out of the pew and waits for Maggie to walk before him. Maggie is asking for God's blessing today and on these men always as she approaches Sr. Jeanne and lifts her cupped hands to receive communion. She remembers receiving communion from nuns in high school and feels warmed by the memory.

Kneeling next to Sean in this tiny chapel named for his mother feels surreal, and she is grateful she did not miss this. She blesses herself after her prayers and turns toward Sean to find him watching her. She covers her mouth from view of anyone in front of them and proceeds to stick her tongue out at him. He sits back shaking his head, doing his best not to burst out laughing.

As soon as Sr. Jeanne says, "Go in peace to love and serve the Lord." Sean signals for Maggie to follow him out. As they hit the hallway, he says, "You'll be hitting confession for that little stunt in church, Maggie." And she quickly replies, "Well, I think you'll be hitting it for a lot more than that."

Sean takes her back to the front desk, where a volunteer makes a copy of her license. Sr. Jeanne meets them there and offers to give Maggie a tour after breakfast. Sean navigates Maggie through the crowd of men lining up in a corridor waiting to enter the breakfast hall. Maggie smiles gently at those that make eye contact with her.

Sean opens a windowed door to the kitchen, warmly greeted by a chef and dishwasher.

"I brought backup, gentlemen. This is Maggie, and she knows her way around a kitchen. Maggie, this is Troy and Miguel."

Maggie shakes both their hands quickly, and Troy takes her to the dish up line where three nuns, a cop, and the deacon are already in place. Troy asks if she is comfortable on the grill with hash browns and pork roll, and Maggie says, "Piece a cake," and ties on an apron. Sean appears to be a runner of sorts and is currently filling large brown thermoses with coffee. Maggie fills chafing dishes with potatoes and works on getting the pork roll into one as well when Sr. Jeanne yells, "Are you ready, Troy?"

She opens the door before Troy can answer, and he laughs and says, "Every day she asks me the same question and does what she wants anyway." Sean looks at Maggie offering, "Imagine that?"

Maggie works her station with a smile and "Good morning" for each of the men. Some respond, while others do not. She focuses on the men in a way others might not, taking in demographics, clothing, and demeanor. Twenty minutes later, she leans over the line and says, "I think we have about ten to twelve to go, Chef."

"Thanks, Maggie, how did you know to tell me that?"

"Just knew, that's all" and gives him a smile. When the line is finished, the nuns ask Maggie to join them for breakfast. She says she will be over in a bit but wants to go around with seconds on coffee since it's so cold out. She grabs two of the glass pour pots by the coffee station, heads to the one-hundred-cup urn, and fills them both. She goes table to table refilling the men's cups and chatting easily with them about the rain, football, the potatoes, anything to fill the void. Some are clearly hungover or coming down from a high. Maggie fills their cups, patting several on their backs as she moves among them.

She sees Sean scrubbing pots and emptying trays with Miguel. He heads toward the tray drop station and spots Maggie laughing with a table of men. He is in awe of her ability to socialize in any setting. He observes her as she makes these men feel valued and cared for in a way that does not patronize them. He feels fortunate to see her in this setting, gaining insight into her character and making him eager for more. Danny comes up from his blind side and asks, "What is she doing here?"

Sean turns and says, "I believe the question is why you are so late?" Danny scoots away quickly.

Maggie sees a man sitting alone near the coffee station. She leaves one pot there, fills the other, and grabs a disposable cup. "Mind if I sit for a minute?" she asks as she fills his cup and pours her own. "My name is Maggie."

"Dennis. Nice to meet you."

Maggie asks him how long he has lived in Rehoboth, and Dennis begins to tell her his story. He looks to be a peer of hers but in reality is thirty-six years old. Maggie listens compassionately with the full understanding that the man exhibits every sign of heroin addiction. Dennis has been between menial jobs for some time, making his way north to find work. He explains his intention to keep moving toward Philly.

Maggie gently warns him, "Stay out of Kensington, Dennis, please. Stay here. At least a few more days until you you've had more to eat and rest."

With that, Dennis gives her a gap-toothed smile and says, "You gonna be back in a few days?"

"I will," lies Maggie. "I'll be looking for you."

She returns her coffee pots to the dish station and looks for Sean. Sr. Jeanne has him cornered by the walk-in freezer. Maggie weighs rescuing him versus watching him squirm from whatever pressure the nun is putting on him. In the end, she decides to make her way over to them. Maggie finds the relief in his eyes as he sees her heading his way humorous. She beats Sr. Jeanne at her own game by speaking first, "How about that tour, Jeanne?"

"Would love to, dear. Do you mind, Sean?"

"No way I'm leaving you two alone. Let me tell Miguel I'm leaving, and I'll catch up."

Sr. Jeanne explains the two wings of the building. One wing accommodates the short-stay, overnight guests. Maggie notices that there are army cots in one large room and another section with bunk beds. A sign indicates the entrance to showers and a delousing room. Sr. Jeanne explains when the men arrive, they turn over their belongings. The men under any kind of influence sleep in the area with the cots. She goes on to explain that the bunks are for sober men simply because they are less likely to fall out of bed. Trained staff oversee each of these areas throughout the night. Bathroom and showers are open areas. Sr. Jeanne explains, "We do our best to move those suffering from addiction to treatment centers, but it's not always possible."

Separating the wings is a large sculpture that Maggie immediately recognizes as Tony's work. The next wing houses longer-term residents. "Sean raised the money to have these dorm rooms fully furnished. We have started a job training and placement service with the men in residence and have an 80 percent placement record. We help them get on their feet and find subsidized housing. We throw them the lifeline, and they pull themselves to safety."

Maggie is impressed with the program but wonders about the other 20 percent. Sean has joined them at this point, explaining the complexities of job training and placement in a seasonal economy. His remarks remind her of their conversation over ice cream. When he details a budding partnership with the University of Delaware's Lewes campus, Maggie talks to him about her contacts at Wilmington University and trades like Delaware Learning Institute of Cosmetology. They immediately begin brainstorming on connections that could help expand the training to include educational goals and opportunities. All the while Sr. Jeanne is taking them in and making mental notes to share with the sisters later.

As they walk down the hall, the dormitory reminds her of those her children lived in on their various campuses. At the end of the hall, there is a heavily decorated door, and as Maggie gets closer, she sees the name Danny in hand-painted letters. She turns to Sean and says, "Danny? Like, our Danny?"

Sr. Jeanne asks, "Oh, how do you know Danny?"

"Long story" is all Sean quickly offers.

Sr. Jeanne explains to Maggie that Danny has lived at the shelter since he was fourteen. His mother was in contact for a while, but that ended before he was sixteen. "The dorm rooms had been finished, but he lived in a room between two of our sisters until he was eighteen. He now has a job at the front desk and helps with meals, especially Sunday breakfast. He's an adult now and has some part-time work at the Purple Parrot, but they seem to call him last minute quite frequently."

"Mmm-hmm." Maggie nods. When Sr. Jeanne picks up a fallen decoration, Maggie leans into Sean. "Are you aware of all of this? And again…where is the heads-up?"

"He's fine, Maggie. He's finding his way. It's not been an easy road for him."

Sr. Jeanne is looking at the two of them with keen interest as Maggie mouths the words "Bullshit" to Sean, walks up to Danny's door, and knocks on it loudly.

Danny cracks open the door, sees Maggie, and is unsure of what to say, so he offers a weak, "Hi, Maggie."

"Well, hello, Danny. Were you at breakfast today, because I didn't see you? I can't believe you wouldn't come up and say hello."

"We were so busy, who had time?"

Sean reminds him, "Some of us were busier than others because people missed their shifts."

Maggie pushes the door open a little wider and says, "I think we need to have a little chat, Danny. Are we doing that in the hall, or are you going to invite me into your room?"

"We are not allowed to have guests."

Maggie reaches behind Danny's arm and pinches it just above his elbow to produce, "Oww!"

"Get moving, mister, unless you need me to remind you about those seagulls." As Danny comes into the hallway, Maggie continues, "Are you being responsible, Danny? For example, did you bother to tell anyone where you were Friday night?"

"No, but—"

"But nothing. Do you see this woman?" Maggie is pointing at Sr. Jeanne. "I'm sure she was up worrying and praying over you. In addition, did you think to send her a text, let alone call her? No, because you were too busy having a great time for yourself. That's pretty disrespectful in my book…almost as bad as not showing up to work when you live here!"

Danny is looking downward and mumbles, "I'm sorry."

"Don't tell me, tell her."

Danny apologizes to Sr. Jeanne thinking the worst has passed. Maggie continues, "You are too old for this, Danny. You need to get it together. You know why, because the only person you can count on in this life is yourself. You have a talent, and you're wasting it when you should be pursuing a certification and license in cosmetology."

"Maggie, I don't have any money."

"There are scholarships available, Danny. And there are benefactors in this world that like to support young people with dreams." She softens, "You can do this. I will leave some information with Sr. Jeanne, and if you are willing to do the research and fill out the applications, I will help you find scholarships."

"You will?"

"Yes, but you have to do the work."

Danny is near tears. "Maggie, will you be my mother?"

"Hell no, I've already raised three kids, but I will be your friend, okay?"

"Okay."

Maggie leans in puts her arm around him to move a few steps away from the others and whispers to him, "And you have to stop prostituting yourself, or I'm out."

"What? How did you—"

"A young man exits a hotel on the boardwalk in the middle of the day with a fist full of twenties and disheveled appearance…it's not rocket science. And while I'm at it, let me see your arms."

Danny quickly rolls up his sleeves and says, "I'm clean, Maggie, I swear."

She gives him a hug and says, "Stay that way. I'll see you tonight."

"Maggie, don't tell the others, okay?"

"I won't today, Danny, but I will when we get home. You don't need a mother, you need a pack of them, and you may just have found them."

After exchanging emails with Sr. Jeanne and promising to send her trade school materials for Danny, Maggie asks Sean if they should get going. The rain falls in torrents, thoroughly soaking them as they run to the Jeep. Once inside, Sean asks, "Was that you as a parent or you in your nonprofit role?"

Maggie watches the windshield wipers rhythmically pushing the water to little avail, concern entering her psyche. "Both, actually. Sean, promise me you will not let him be a slacker because you feel badly for him. It's not fair to him."

He reaches for her hand. "I promise, but I'm no you."

She withdraws her hand and looks directly at him. "And you understand you're going to pay for his education if he does what I advise him to do, right?"

He responds without hesitation, "I assumed as much, but it has to be anonymous."

"That's for you and Sr. Jeanne to figure out."

Something in her demeanor has begun to change, causing him to ask, "And where will you be in all this?"

Maggie looks at the rain outside her window and softly says, "Pennsylvania."

CHAPTER 16

Out on a Limb

Sean swings the Jeep into his usual spot at Darby's and explains that he needs to quickly check on the building given all the rain. Maggie is wet and cold and asks to stay in the car, provided he will not be too long. As Sean unlocks the kitchen door, Maggie takes out her phone and looks at the time, 11:10. She knows that she will be back in Pennsylvania in twenty-four hours and rubs her chest in an attempt to calm her anxiety.

She quickly tests Jen. "I suck as a friend…will be back by 3."
Ping. **Do NOT worry about it c u soon.**

She spies Sean pacing in the restaurant kitchen, talking on the phone. Maggie googles Darby's and checks the Sunday dining hours, "Sunday dinner, only 5–10." She assumes he will need to be back by three. As that thought registers, Sean is back in the Jeep. "You okay?"

"Just cold, I think."

"Not buying that, but let's go back to my place. A hot shower, some lunch, and a fire will do you good."

She avoids making eye contact with him, replying, "No fire, Sean, I'm running out of time. I need to get back to the girls and catch up on plans for tonight."

Sean drives the ten blocks home in silence. Maggie's mood continues to darken, frustrating him. Once in the house, Maggie heads upstairs and starts to pull her things together. Sean takes a reluctant Rosie outside before climbing the steps to his bedroom. He enters to find Maggie zipping up her bag and says, "So that's it. You just want to pack it up and shut it down?"

118

Again, she avoids eye contact, keeping her head down as she answers, "What do you want from me, Sean? The reality of this situation is not good. This is—"

"Stop. Stop right now. You're not doing this yet." Sean comes toward her, takes her bag, and throws it across the room. "There are two of us in this, Maggie, you might want to remember that."

With that, he pulls her to him, kisses her aggressively as he puts his hands through her rain-soaked hair to hold her head, and says, "Tell me you really don't want me now, in this moment, and I'll drive you back, or you stay and we—"

She gives him no chance to finish his sentence as she covers his mouth with hers and begins tearing off his clothes.

*****

On the south end of the island, in a beach house that has been their home for four days, Maggie's friends are lounging. Jen pops down on the sectional next to Laci to tell the group she has received a cryptic update from Maggie. The women are quick to agree that Maggie is feeling guilty for no reason.

Laci responds to the group, "She's twisted. She has been part of everything except sleeping here. And if I were her, I would dump our asses in heartbeat. I mean, he's hot for an old guy."

"You may want to edit that last part when she returns," adds Cassie.

Emily asks, "Jen, you're the closest to her. What's our strategy here?"

"I don't know. I'm tempted to call Caroline and have her talk her mother off the ledge. She's going to blow this unless someone can get inside her head."

"No!" Laci is up and pacing. "No twenty-something wants to deal with their mother's sex life. Hell, I'm thirty-something and still don't want to hear about it, although my mother insists on filling me in."

A collective groan comes from the others. Laci offers, "We have to be ready when she gets back. We need a busy Maggie. We need something to occupy that complicated brain of hers, and then she will open up about her feelings."

The women settle on focusing Maggie's mind on the drag show. Laci has been rehearsing the few moves she and Danny discussed, with Emily as her Danny stand-in, but feels like she should enhance her role. The conversation has taken a turn toward the ridiculous as they debate the use of props and embellishments.

Emily asks, "Did anyone pack a vibrator?"

"That would be a first," says Jen.

Laci cannot help herself. "Maybe it would and maybe it wouldn't."

Cassie suggests Laci channel Julie Andrews in Victor/Victoria for her look, and Laci begins texting Danny, who approves wholeheartedly with the direction they are going in. He informs Laci of a nine-o'clock arrival backstage. She and Danny are scheduled for ten thirty, which will likely mean eleven o'clock. After the texting slows, Jen asks, "And exactly how are we busying the matriarch with all of this?"

Laci is quick to explain, "Because Maggie will kick it up a notch, and we all go along because it's usually brilliant and all inclusive. It will happen organically."

Emily looks concerned. "Speaking of organically, I think we need to do a pulse check when she comes in. If she needs to talk, we may need to listen first."

Jen is skeptical. "Don't count on it."

*****

Sean pulls on shorts and a T-shirt as Maggie showers. Any frustration he may have had an hour ago has fully dissipated. He is damning her in his head while simultaneously surrendering his heart. She is challenging and captivating at the same time. Never has he been at such a disadvantage in a relationship. He begins to wonder if this is a good thing.

They are so different. Sean does not exhibit emotion easily, especially anger. He values and gives respect only after thorough assessment. He considers Maggie for a moment. Respect? She demands it from the moment you meet her. As for emotions, Kevin was dead wrong. She has an abundance of them anger, compassion, joy, warmth, anxiety, sorrow, affection, and based on his experience, an extra dose of passion that makes her undeniably desirable. However, there is also fear. He knows that emotion could drive her from him.

Their attraction to each other is the strongest he has ever experienced, yet he wonders about the give portion of the give and take that makes for great relationships. As he attempts to wrap his mind around this woman, the bathroom door opens, and she appears, dressed in full denial of what she has done to him. She grabs her bag off the floor by his walk-in closet, brings it to the bed, and picks up where she left off, rummaging through it.

"What are you looking for?"

"My makeup bag."

Sean knows exactly where it is, but he waits for her to make eye contact with him. It is slow coming, but when she does, instead of anger or defensiveness, he sees sorrow. "It's downstairs on the dryer. I'll get it for you."

"That's okay. I'll get it on my way out. Listen, I ordered an Uber. I was surprised you have them down here."

"You ordered an Uber?"

"Yeah, you just download the app and—"

"Maggie, I'm not a hundred, I own a restaurant. I damn well know what it is. The question is why would you do that?"

"Because, Sean, it's time to go. It's almost two o'clock, you've got to get to work, and I should spend time with my friends. It's just easier, that's all."

"That, and you can avoid having a conversation about what tomorrow brings. You, the woman who has been watching the time we have left as if it were a New Year's Eve countdown, is just catching a ride from a stranger rather than let me drive you there. I give up."

"What does that mean?"

"It means I surrender, you win. You want this not to work, then it won't." For a moment, he thinks she is going to cry, but then out of nowhere comes a strength that surprises him, leaving him speechless.

"I think you are being a little dramatic. You know where I will be tonight. The girls are counting on seeing you, especially Laci. We'll see each other at the Parrot."

The bag goes over her shoulder, and she heads for the stairs. As she walks past the kitchen, she looks at the unlit fire and starts to cry. She now knows with full certainty she will never see it lit. She grabs her makeup bag and stuffs it into her duffel. She dries her eyes on her sleeve, pinches her cheeks, and licks her lips.

He is waiting by the front door. Maggie is taken aback by the sight of him, his trademark edginess fully restored, leaving her heart in shambles. She sees a car pull up in front of the house, walks toward Sean, and says, "I… I'll see you tonight."

As she goes to hug him, he stops her and says, "We'll see," opens the door, and turns away as she walks through it.

CHAPTER 17

Mixed Signals

The gray Toyota Camry parks in front of the beach rental. Maggie exits the car, glad the rain is still falling because at least the girls are not hanging on the deck. She thanks and tips the driver and checks the app to make sure the driver has marked the ride as completed.

She takes a deep breath and enters the house with the intention of getting to her room with little to no questions asked. She is numb. How did she allow herself to spend two nights with him? She deeply contemplates the gargantuan mess she has made as she reaches the top of the stairs. Emily is the first to see her, giving her that sweet, reassuring smile they all adore. "Hey, Mags, did you have lunch?"

"Actually, no, and now that you mention it, I'm starving."

"I'll bet you are," teases Laci.

Maggie weakly shakes her head and walks back to her the bedroom to drop her bag and put on her yoga pants and a Tufts crew team hoodie. The minute she shuts the door of the bedroom, the women are up and in the kitchen with Emily. "Shit, this is not good," says Laci. "Jen, go ask her if she's okay."

"No way, not poking the bear."

Emily shoos them out of the kitchen and tells someone to open some wine because it could be a long afternoon. As Emily warms tomato bisque and quickly makes a grilled cheese for Maggie, she decides the bear needs lunch and a good old-fashioned poking. Maggie enters the great room and smells the grilled cheese. "Oh my god, Em, you are a lifesaver."

"Go sit down on the couch. I'll bring it to you. I've opened the Markham. Want some?"

Just being in the presence of these women has restored her humor. "Is Bradley Cooper a stud?"

Maggie is savoring every dip of the grilled cheese in the soup. And after three quarters of it has been eagerly consumed, she looks at the four of them and says, "What's with the silence?"

Jen turns to Cassie. "C'mon, Cassie, we better pull a few bottles from the cooler. I sense an intervention coming on."

Laci yells "Chickenshits!" as they scamper down the stairs. "Maybe we should take this to the hot tub."

"Not yet, Lace, I just got warm," says Maggie. "But I do need more wine." Maggie pours herself another glass, and Emily raises an eyebrow in Laci's direction. Jen and Cassie are heading up the steps with two Markham chardonnays and two Cloudy Bay sauvignon blancs. Maggie allows them all settle back in their seats before saying, "You are the biggest wimps I've ever met... Go ahead, ask!"

Emily starts, "First of all, great dinner party, Mags. I don't think we've ever done that before."

Jen adds, "Oh my god, remember the time Maggie invited half the bar at the Baja to brunch the next day in Virginia Beach?"

Maggie is laughing at herself. "Those Southern boys and girls were scared to death of us. What were we drinking that night?"

Cassie meekly says, "Lemon drops," and they all start laughing.

Maggie stretches out, and Laci curls up next to her. "Oh god, here it comes," Maggie sighs with a smile as she hugs the youngest of her beloved pack. "Let me have it because I know it's going to be about our favorite subject." Maggie and Laci proclaimed themselves as the sluts of the group several trips ago, although they both know their friends have very healthy libidos.

"So exactly what is going on over at Sean's house, Maggie? Like how many times, where, is he out of practice or primed and ready to go, and while you're at it—"

Maggie interrupts, "You really are a freak. Do you think you should call Dex, have a little phone sex, and come back when you're ready to handle the conversation?"

"Aww, girl, it was that hot?"

"I'm going to take it from the top, but the cliff notes version, and then entertain questions at the end." Maggie gives a quick recap up to going for ice cream last night and going back to Sean's house, but for Laci's benefit, she teases, "You know how there's all kinds of sex, not just positions, right?"

Laci encourages a further explanation, "Like?"

"Well, when you're married, sometimes it's just an obligatory cardiovascular activity, right?"

They are all nodding and laughing. Maggie is holding court now and continues, "And then there's the 'let's do it under the Christmas tree because we just did all of this for our kids' sex."

Now Emily joins in, "One year JT and I did it between the bikes he just finished building at three in the morning."

Jen adds, "Maybe I do want kids."

Maggie smiles in Laci's direction. "Well, last night was…"

Laci is hanging on every word, as Maggie continues, "No sex."

Emily gushes, "You opened up, didn't you? You talked all night, right? I'm so proud of you."

"Don't be that proud." Maggie then launches into a recap of the evening, a high level mention of sharing some details about her childhood, including her brother's passing, the storm blowing in, and her basically passing out from exhaustion.

"I'm still proud of you," says Emily as she fills her wineglass and tops Maggie's and Laci's.

Maggie continues, "Well then, today just got…kind of weird. No, not kind of weird, another planet weird."

Laci leans in. "Were there costumes involved?"

"Please go call Dex. You need it, girl. Oh, wait a minute, it's been more than seventy-two hours since you two have had sex, which explains it. I'll go on."

Maggie details the morning at the shelter and tour of the facility. She fights the temptation to tell them about Danny but remembers her promise. She talks about her observations of Sean with his friends, Jim, Scott, and Larry, his staff, his chemistry with his well-trained dog, and the peace he exhibited when in the shelter this morning. She omits telling them about naming it after his brother and the sweet little chapel dedicated to his mother. She speaks of the sculpture that moved Maggie more than she knew until she described its presence in the middle of the facility.

"The fluidity of Tony's work is both sensual and serene. There are elements of nature reflected in the two pieces I've seen, one water, the other captures prisms of light, leaving a ring of sparkles around its base where the light hits it. It's captivating in a place that could be so depressing."

"Maggie, this is not that weird. This is you we are talking about here, of course you went to the shelter," says Jen as she holds her wineglass out for a refill from Cassie.

"Oh, I'm getting to it." She talks about leaving and their conversation in the car about one of the younger regulars going to school and Sean setting up an anonymous scholarship. She is in the middle of her story and fails to notice the curiosity from her friends about Sean's ability to do so. Instead, she remains lost in recapping their exchange as if unknowingly identifying a tipping point in her emotions. "And then he asked me where I would be when all this came to fruition, and it hit me like a ton of bricks. All I could say was... Pennsylvania."

She explains waiting outside the restaurant when she sent Jen the text, the quiet ride back to his house, and the realization that came over her. She reviews going up to pack her bag, which led to, "So he comes upstairs after quite a bit of time and is like 'What are you doing?'"

Emily puts her head in her hands, thinking, *Sean, I told you not to leave her alone.*

Maggie is now speaking directly to Laci and says, "And then the fool has the nerve to try and give me an ultimatum, but rather than hear him out, I just fucked him...or maybe he just fucked me, but whichever, there was a huge undercurrent to it. You know what I mean?"

Laci is pondering the question like a scientist examining a specimen. "I'm pulling together the evidence and coming to my hypothesis." She pauses. "Would you say it was more like alpha female power sex or…was it goodbye sex?"

"Goodbye sex?" asks Cassie.

Laci explains, "Yeah, not just the sending your guy on the road for a business trip sex where you want him to think, 'Damn, my wife is hot, I can't wait to get home.'"

Professor Laci, faux PhD in sexual behavior, pauses for effect. "Goodbye sex is the 'I'm never going to get to do this again, so we're gonna do it till we leave a mark on each other's souls that's as permanent as a tattoo' kind of sex. It's the sex you'll remember for the rest of your life."

Maggie stands up, grabs a wine bottle, turns to Laci with tears in her eyes, and says, "Yeah, that one."

"Oh, honey." Laci leaps up, takes the wine bottle, and hands it to Emily as she wraps her in a hug, and waves on the others so that one by one, the women join in and engulf her.

Maggie gasps for air and breaks free of the group hug. "Screw him! It's hot tub time, ladies."

*****

"I'm dramatic. Did you know that, Rosie? I'm dramatic." Sean is grabbing used towels from the bathroom to take to the laundry room when a hair tie falls on the floor. "Why do I feel I'm going to find traces of her for weeks?"

Rosie gives her owner a quizzical look before jumping onto his bed, where she promptly sniffs the pillow Maggie slept on and curls herself beneath it so that she can lay her head where Maggie's once was.

"Traitor."

Sean takes the towels downstairs and starts the washer. He shakes his head when he finds the bottle of rosewater she uses in her hair absently left on the dryer. As he walks through the front of the house, he sees Jim wrestling with returning his porch chair to its previous position. He heads out to help him. The rain is starting to ease up, but the winds are still blowing with gusts of twenty-plus miles per hour. As he jogs over, he yells, "Whoa, what are you doing, old man?"

Jim stops what he is doing and turns to greet his friend. "Some hooligan pulled a prank on me last night and brought my outdoor furniture inside the house. Looks like he has returned to the scene of the crime."

Sean steps in front of him and easily lifts the rocker through the doorway and places it on the porch. "We've talked about this. You are supposed to text me, remember?"

"I was actually hoping you were otherwise occupied."

Sean looks at his watch and says, "Let's go in. Storm's not over yet." He and Jim head to the kitchen, where Jim pours him a cup of coffee from the twenty-year-old Mr. Coffee Pot that still "works perfectly well." Sean asks if Jim has had lunch yet and is happy to hear he has not. "Good, I'm starved. I'll make it."

As Sean rummages around the refrigerator, Jim suggests, "There's ham and swiss in the deli drawer, mustard on the door, and rye bread on the bottom shelf."

"That'll work," says Sean as he secretly checks expiration dates on things in the fridge. He feels proud of his friend. This bachelor life is more than what he bargained for, and he does his best to stay on top of the things Eileen always took care of for him. Sean toasts the rye, slaps together the sandwiches, finds a bag of Herr's potato chips and pickles. and lunch is ready.

As Sean sits down at the kitchen table, Jim takes a bite of his sandwich and says, "It's always better when someone else makes it for you." Sean's mind drifts to Friday night when Maggie surprised him by making him something to eat after what had been a very long day. He cannot remember the last time someone had done that for him.

Jim looks at the man he considers to be like a son, analyzes his distracted demeanor, and asks, "What's troubling you, Sean?"

Sean offers one word: "Maggie."

"You'll have to give me more than that, or I won't be able to help you."

Sean considers shutting down on the subject, but as he sips his coffee, his eye catches a black-and-white photo of Eileen on the wall by the staircase at the opposite end of the kitchen. In it, Eileen is on the beach, wrapped in a traditional Irish plaid wool scarf, full skirt, and stark white blouse. She is challenging the photographer with a devilish look in her eyes and an innocent smile. Sean points to it and asks, "Who took that picture of her?"

Jim replies, "I did. We had just finished midterms at Penn, and I somehow managed to convince her to spend the weekend with me down here."

Sean smiles. "You sly dog."

"Yes, I was. Now what does that photo have to do with Maggie?"

"There are some similarities, that's all. I'm afraid it doesn't matter though, Jim. She's gone."

When Jim remains quiet, Sean begins to fill in some of the events of the past few days. Jim laughs heartily at the swim in the cold ocean and the tantrum in the parking lot with the woman who spoke ill of her. Conversely, he gets sentimental when he learns of them sharing their tales of grief and personal growth. When Sean describes her at the shelter and the mood shift by the time they returned home, he admits to knowing she was slipping away.

"Of course she was," consoles Jim. "It's overwhelming to think you've met your match when you don't have enough time to be sure it's true. Another thing, a woman like Maggie wants to think she has the upper hand. Trust me on that one. Conversely, you can't just let her have it, because she also wants a man strong enough to challenge her when she needs it or she'll become bored. It's a delicate dance, my boy."

"Yes, it is."

Sean clears the plates and loads them in the dishwasher as Jim states, "I thought she told me she was leaving on Monday."

"She is."

"Well then, she's not gone yet. Here's what you need to do…"

Sean listens intently as Jim offers a few strategies and encourages him to focus on getting to one specific, achievable outcome: to continue the relationship. "Worry less about the specifics of how it will continue. Let her fill in those details. She has to feel like she is not just wanted, but that she is also in control, because she is. Leave your ego at the door, man, and good luck."

*****

Maggie wonders, what is it about cramming into a hot tub with four other women that soothes her nerves and washes away her worries? Is it the warmth, the bubbles, the pulsing on her weary lower back…*splash!* Jen continues to agitate Maggie with water and begins, "No more wine for you until you sober up a bit. We need your brain around something."

"I do my best thinking when I'm half lit. There will be no sobering up anytime soon. Reality hits tomorrow. I'm not living in the moment. I choose to live in the land of denial. Now, what's up?" Maggie grabs a water pistol from the side of the hot tub and squirts it in her mouth.

Laci is intrigued. "Yo, Mags, what's in there?"

"Open up." Maggie proceeds to squirt champagne into Laci's mouth. Laci steals the toy and starts making the rounds with the other women.

"This is genius. Why have we not thought about this before now?"

"Stress makes me highly creative, and I am under a shit ton of stress right now, that's why. Jen, what's the dilemma?"

"How many times will any of us be in a drag show, right? The occasion calls for a personal best from all of us, but we're stalled." Jen gets a read on Maggie. She seems more intent on the champagne shooter than taking Jen's bait.

"Tell me what you've got so far."

As Jen launches into the current plan, Maggie begins to ask for details about costumes, the dimensions of the stage, the music, and the average crowd at the Parrot on a Sunday night. Maggie mulls over details, thinks about Jen's skills, and says, "Look, it sounds great, and you don't really need to add anything…but you could consider ramping up the marriage equality angle."

Jen and Maggie begin brainstorming, and thirty minutes later, they are all out of the hot tub and pulling together materials for their political statement. Maggie donates a white sheet from the bed she has barely slept in. Emily has pulled together every marker she can find. Cassie has pulled a list of hashtags for Jen's review. Jen syncs up their phones and creates a social media strategy and assignment for each woman. Cassie has Facebook, Jen has Instagram, Maggie's on Twitter, and Emily will mastermind YouTube.

When Laci asks, "What about me? Don't I need one?"

Jen answers, "Sweetie, you're the eye of the storm. Just keep Danny happy and camera ready. If we get this thing out with a little momentum, I'll need you to like, share, and hashtag after the performance because you have the widest Instagram network."

They decide to use #marriageequality and #supremecourt and type it in their notes field and in a group text to one another so that it will be an easy copy and paste. Jen and Maggie discuss arriving at the Parrot early to commandeer a table. She then places a call to the owner of the Purple Parrot to vet their plans. She ends the call with a confident smile, a warm thank you, and a thumbs-up to her friends. Feeling prepared, the women begin to get ready for their last night out.

Maggie is dressed first, waiting on a free bathroom to do her makeup. She has put on her dark wash jeans, a black scoop neck T-shirt, and purple-and-blue paisley pashmina scarf. As she plays with her scarf in the reflection of the sliding glass door, her phone vibrates in her pocket. It's a missed call from Patrick. Maggie decides to head back to her room to call him back.

"Hey, Mom, what's up?"

Maggie begins by telling him about their plans for the drag show and asks that he keep his phone near him between ten thirty and eleven thirty tonight. She explains the plan to get some social media buzz around it to bring more attention to the impending Supreme Court ruling scheduled for some time in 2015.

"Mom, please tell me you're not in charge of the social media or the photos."

Maggie is smiling at her son's candor. "Not to worry, Jen has it all under control. I've been assigned to Twitter feed, and I wrote and scheduled most of that already. Oh, and I helped with the banner."

"Sounds great, Mom, count me in. I will give a few other people a heads-up about it too. I've never been jealous of your girls' weekend, but I kind of am this year. I mean, my mother at a drag show. I'm not gonna lie, I'm kind of proud. So have fun and—"

Maggie interrupts him, "Patrick, do you have a few minutes?"

"Always. You okay?"

"Umm, it's just that, well, I've met someone."

"Hey, isn't that usually my line?"

"I guess so, but it's true, and I could really use someone to talk to."

"I'm sorry, Mom, you're serious. Let me walk into the next room. I'm all yours."

Rather than give a recap of the last three days, Maggie chooses to talk about the man she has learned so much about over such a short time. She talks about his character, intellect, conviction, apparent amusement over her volatility, and dark mystique. Patrick asks when they met, and she talks about the introduction on the beach on day one but leaves out his cocky "Text me" move.

"I don't know, Pat, he's got a lot of layers, and I kind of don't. What you see is what you get with me. He's guarded, and I'm completely transparent."

"What? No, you are not! I mean yes, at work, Mom, but as far as your personal life goes, you are comp-li-cated! But I'm not sure I understand what's bothering you."

"Am I too old for this? I keep asking myself, 'What am I doing?' I'm leaving tomorrow, and I still don't know the answer to that question."

"All right, let me recap. You met this person four days ago, and you're not talking about what he does for a living or how many times you've seen him… You're just telling me the kind of person he is. What I'm hearing is that you respect him, are intrigued by him, and that he has gotten inside your head. Wow… Okay, I have to ask you a few questions. Just give me quick answers. Is he older or younger than you?"

Maggie tries to hide her amusement over the phone, but she finds her son's protective instincts endearing. "A little older...like four years older."

"So you know his birthday?"

"I do." Maggie remembers asking Sean that before she fell asleep last night and her heart constricts.

"Does he have a job?"

"Oh my god, Patrick, yes!"

"Just checking, Mom. I mean, I can't exactly get down there and size this guy up." He is hesitating. Maggie is curious to see what could possibly be next.

"Have your friends spent time with him?"

"Yes, and all favorable opinions, as favorable as four days can get you anyway."

"Last one, I am going to assume as two middle-aged adults, you've been responsible, but I also assume you've probably had some kind of sex by now. So is there anything amiss or weird going on there?"

Maggie can't help herself. She breaks into all out laughter before replying, "No blue pills, no weird requests or fetishes. Geez, Patrick, you must think your mother can only attract creepy, unemployed forty- or seventy-something-year-olds waiting to take advantage of her."

"Pardon me for caring. So to answer your question...you are not too old for this. Frankly, it is about time. And as for what you are doing, well, Mom, whether you like it or not, you've started a relationship with this guy."

"I guess I have, but I also think I may have screwed it up."

"Does that upset you, or do you not care?"

"No, I care."

"Then apologize."

"Thanks, Patrick. You know I love you, right?"

"Love you too, Mom. See you next weekend. Good luck tonight."

Maggie loves her children equally, but tonight, the gratitude she feels for her son knows no limits. That conversation would have lasted four hours with her daughters and gotten nowhere. Maggie opens her text app and finds Sean listed under Jen's from earlier today. She hits his name, and the conversation trail opens.

She types, "Im sorry."

She shoves her phone in her pocket before she can see if he is writing a response. She grabs her makeup bag and heads into the bathroom, where Jen is finishing up. Maggie can tell that Jen has her game face on, which means this is really going down.

"Was that my favorite college hunk on the phone with you?"

"Yup, trying to coach his mother on tonight. He is on standby and pulling in some of his friends. We'll need the college kids to give this traction."

"What about the girls?"

"They'll see it from him, and then it's out to their networks. It's all crazy to me, but let's have fun with it."

As they high five, Maggie's pocket vibrates. She waits for Jen to take her things back to their room before she opens her phone.

For?

Maggie hates this. She is not great at the apology thing, but before she can resent Sean for pushing her to explain, she types.

For being an ass and calling Uber. It was not nice.

Thank you, not my finest hour either.

Maggie's heart melts, and she almost types what she was going to say to him at the door but decides to wait until she sees him.

We r leaving in 5—will u get there?

Closing early we will all be there.

Maggie is smiling as she goes back to her room and informs Jen that Darby's is closing early so staff can come down. Jen gives Maggie a knowing smile and says, "Why do I think I'm sleeping alone again tonight?"

Maggie throws her pillow at her friend and replies, "I should be so lucky."

They head down the hall to join the others in time to hear the traditional pregame pop of champagne.

CHAPTER 18

These Are My People

The storm has officially passed by the time the women head out. Emily finds a parking spot three blocks from the Purple Parrot, and the women pile out of the car at precisely eight forty-five. Laci exhibits no sign of nerves. She doesn't have time because Danny has been texting her nonstop for twenty minutes.

Laci sports her thigh-high boots, sequined shorts, and a white halter while carrying her black pinstriped suit and the wedding dress in her garment bag for later tonight. Jen is dressed for battle, celadon fine knit sweater with a bejeweled neckline, skinny jeans. Her black flak jacket has pockets jammed with phone chargers, markers, and God knows what else. Cassie is three paces ahead of everyone but easily identified in black jeans and an electric blue flutter sleeve blouse. Maggie feeds the meter as Emily checks and locks her car. She chose a blush-pink peplum blouse with a gray cashmere wrap over her citizen jeans.

"Damn if we all don't look good," says Maggie as they link arms and follow the others toward the uplit yellow building with the purple door and blue awning. Emily insisted Maggie tweak her outfit before they left. She advised, "Let's go, Maggie, a little less mom and little more you, hot stuff." Off went the scarf in favor of her crescent moon necklace, black-and-gold wrap bracelet, drop earrings, and leopard-print heels.

"Glad you lost the scarf in favor of the heels. Think Sean will notice them?"

"Every man with a pulse does."

As Maggie and Emily enter the bar, they see an already-packed house. Cassie informs them they are to wait at the entrance. A handsome, brown-eyed forty-something man enters the bar area by way of the kitchen donning a backward baseball hat and Purple Parrot apron. He walks up to the women and flashes a dazzling smile as he asks, "Is Laci here?"

Laci takes a dramatic step into the center of the conversation circle. "Yup, reporting for duty."

"I'm Andrew Fletcher. Thanks for doing this." He continues to beam at each of them, sends a sly smile toward one of them, and continues, "You must be Maggie. Sean described you perfectly. He called and asked that I save you all a table. It's packed, and I could only save one."

Maggie shakes Andrew's hand. "No problem, Andrew. We'll be on the dance floor until showtime anyway. We'll have plenty of seats."

"Who's Jen?"

"Right here," replies Jen. "What do you need?"

"Come on back with me. We'll drop Laci off at the dressing room, and then I can show you the best vantage point for photos." He hands her a zip drive. "The logo as jpeg, png, and eps, along with other marketing materials that are on here."

"You're making this easy for me. Thanks, Andrew!"

Jen walks back to the table around nine fifteen to find Scott and Larry seated with Emily and Cassie. "Where the hell is Maggie?" she asks.

Cassie points to the far end of the bar. "Already found someone she knows and is chatting away, per usual. One of her brother's friends or something. Did you see Laci backstage?"

"Oh my god, yes. These queens have officially abducted our girl. She whispered in my ear before I left, 'These are my people,' leaned back, and let the makeup and hair crew have their way with her. They were getting ready to cut her hair. I left as they were debating what color to make it... Could be purple, could be jet black. Who knows?"

Maggie saunters back to the table all smiles and announces, "I've been friending people at the bar. Hey, Jen, could use your help, pal. Between the two of us, we could add another fifty to seventy to our network. How much longer till showtime?"

Scott and Larry have arrived. Scott suggests they wrap it up in thirty minutes or they may not make it back to the table. Before Maggie can turn and scoot, Jen pulls her aside to tell her there is a problem with the photo angle. Andrew had wanted to use a surveillance camera, but Jen feels it will take too long to download and edit the image.

Maggie looks at the stage and peers around the room. "You only have one option, Jen. You are going up on that bar. Do you think you can get it from there?"

Jen eyes the distance, the angles, and the probability of finding an open spot. "It's not a slam dunk. I'll be okay if I can get up there, but who's going clear the way?"

Maggie smiles confidently. "Tall, dark, and edgy...with some help from Jesse and Mac. What's the run time on 'Believe'?"

Larry pipes in out of nowhere, "Three minutes, forty-two seconds." Jen and Maggie smirk at each other.

"All right then, we have a game plan," answers Jen. "I need a drink. How about you, Maggie?"

They move through the thickening crowd to squeeze through a space at the bar. Maggie orders a fresh vodka cranberry for Jen and a shot of Patron for herself. The female bartender delivers up the order, and as Maggie is about to tip her, she hears her say to the barback, "Well, look what the cat dragged in. Gonna be a good night for me after all."

Maggie turns toward the entrance as she hands Jen her drink to see Sean talking with Andrew. Jen witnesses the quick pivot back toward the bar. Maggie leans in, hands the bartender a twenty dollars, and snarls, "Back off, bitch."

Jen quickly grabs Maggie's elbow, pulls her away from the bar, and says, "Numero uno, you have nothing to worry about, secondly, no more tequila until you've done your job, and thirdly, please do not get us thrown out of here."

Maggie scowls in Jen's direction, downs her shot, and gives her a "Fine."

Becca strides over to them as soon as she spots them heading their way. She is bubbling over. "Oh my god, I'm so excited. They've never had a woman in the drag show before! How can I help?"

Maggie and Jen talk to her about getting Jen up on the bar. Becca suggests they go from behind the bar, explaining that restaurant people take care of their own and she will be able to find someone to help. It's decided that Jesse and Mac are the best ones to get Jen back there, but Sean should clear it with Andrew. When Becca heads back to Sean, Maggie and Jen see both Sean and Andrew nodding in agreement. Andrew gives them a thumbs-up from the door. Sean looks up from Becca and spots Maggie. No smile, just that piercing stare.

Emily arrives beside her friends, looks at Sean, and says, "Geez, Mags, and that's kind of intense. No wonder you were a little off your game this afternoon. Jen, I just got a text from Laci. They start in ten minutes. She and Danny are the fifth act in, probably twenty minutes out."

Jen reviews where Emily and Cassie should stand. Emily confirms that she has the banner in her bag at the table, and Scott is watching over it. Jen tells Maggie to send out her teaser tweets every five minutes until she sees Danny and Laci hit the stage. Maggie is using the tweet "Do you believe in love?" followed by hashtags of famous openly gay men and women.

Maggie wiggles her finger at Sean to get him to come over to her. He shakes his head no and holds up his Rolex-clad wrist indicating time to pay attention. Becca is now by her side. "Maggie, let me help."

Maggie understands tonight is all about casting a wide net and is happy to have a young thirty-something working beside her. They quickly follow each other across various mediums. She notices that Becca add Darby's as well. She thinks, *Smart girl*, and wonders if Sean knows what he has in her. As the DJ stops and the dance floor clears, Becca leans closer to Maggie and quietly says, "You're the best thing that's ever happened to him."

Maggie says, "I don't know, I guess we'll see about that. Becca, who's the bitch behind the bar, and what's their history?"

"No history, although she wishes. Take a look in the mirror, Maggie, there's no contest."

Maggie sees an opening, grabs Becca, and says, "Follow me, we are getting as close to the stage as possible."

The evening's emcee, Ms. Sea Shell, slinks out to warm up the crowd. She swings past Maggie, looks at her feet, and announces to the audience, "Someone follow her home. I need those shoes."

Maggie gives her a wink and blows her a kiss. Sea Shell flirts her way across the front tables and begins to announce the first act, and Shania Twain's "Man! I Feel Like a Woman!" fills the bar as Farah Moan struts her way across the stage. As the fourth act, Patti No Telle, begins her version of "New Attitude," Maggie peers into the wings to spot six pink taffeta gowns with bouffant dos anxiously awaiting their turn. She tells Becca to get Jen, Mac, and Jesse moving toward Sean and Andrew as quickly as possible.

Laci and Danny are holding hands in the right wing of the stage. Emily and Cassie catch Laci's eye from across the dance floor and give her thumbs-up. Ms. Shell quiets the crowd and begins, "Ladies and gentlemen, tonight the Purple Parrot is breaking with tradition in order to bring some awareness and acceptance into our little world. Please join me in welcoming our first female performer in the history of the Purple Parrot." She pauses to allow the crowd to whoop and cheer. Maggie sees Emily filming with her phone and Cassie screaming.

"We proudly present Ms. Laci Thong and her partner, Ms. Vivienne Veil!" Maggie is laughing so hard she is crying while trying to type in Laci's and Danny's stage names into Twitter. The crowd is roaring as the intro begins and the bridesmaids are released. Cher's voice echoes "After love, after love, after love."

Laci struts out, hot pants, boots, jacket, no shirt, and spiked metallic silver hair replicating Vegas Cher. Maggie catches Jen being lifted on to the bar by the guys as Laci begins lip-syncing her first line, walking up to patrons like she's done this all her life. "No matter how hard I try, you keeping pushing me aside, and I can't break through…"

Laci spots the DC boys at another table and slides into one of their laps, straddles him, and as she leaves their table, she asks two of them to kiss. The bar goes nuts for her.

As she hits "What am I supposed to do sit around and wait for you," Danny comes out in full bridal regalia. He grabs the mic for "I know that I'll get through this. I know that I am strong. I don't need you anymore."

He and Laci are now strutting circles around each other as the bridesmaids form a semicircle around them. As the final verse comes up, the bridesmaids engulf Danny, a wig and veil are tossed to Cassie, and the wedding dress is on the floor. The circle opens to reveal Danny dressed in sequin hot pants, silver sequin cap, and silver-star pasties. The bridesmaids are wearing tear-away dresses that quickly reveal identical costumes, and in a moment of solidarity, Laci tosses her jacket to the crowd to reveal the very same pasties. There is a thunderous reaction from the patrons.

As Laci fades out to "I really don't think you're strong enough now," Emily holds one end of the banner, and Cassie takes the other and runs in front of them revealing the message, "Legalize Same-Sex Marriage #marriageequality #supremecourt." Jen is shooting fast and furiously from atop the bar. People are going nuts, and Maggie swoops in to rescue Laci's wedding dress from the floor before it ends up ripped to pieces. The DJ replays Cher's anthem, and gay men lead the rush to the dance floor.

Maggie lifts her head in time to catch Jen doing a crowd dive off the front of the bar into Mac's and Jesse's waiting arms as they carry her toward the dance floor. Maggie is now on a mission. She makes her way to the table to deposit Laci's dress. The photo comes through her phone, and she and Becca are up and running. Eight furious minutes of typing later, they both sit back and sigh.

"Who did you hashtag, Maggie?"

"Ellen, Elton John, Neil Patrick Harris, Cher, and Lance Bass… you?"

"Chris Colfer, Rosie O'Donnell, Anderson Cooper, and Andy Cohen."

"Sweet!"

Maggie grabs Becca by the hand and leads her to the dance floor to join her friends as the DJ rolls into "It's Raining Men." She and Becca bow to Laci and Danny. Mac and Jesse dance with Jen and Becca. Maggie turns her head toward the entrance and runs to drag Sean onto the dance floor. "Let me see what the nuns taught you, Sean." He is nothing short of amazed by these women and laughing with Maggie, twirling her around as the DJ switches to Aretha Franklin's "Respect."

As they settle back in at the table, drinks arrive courtesy of Andrew. Cassie puts Laci's jacket over her shoulders, which promptly gets shrugged off. "I'm so hot…literally!"

Everyone is taking pictures of Laci and Danny, asking Laci to sign just about everything in sight. Jen pulls Sharpies from her jacket and places them on the table. Danny hands Laci a dollar bill, and she signs it as Laci Thong. They pin it to the wall by the table, where it joins hundreds of others. Laci takes a quick selfie with Danny in front of the dollar.

Maggie grabs a Sharpie and a dollar bill out of her pocket. She writes something on the bill and hands it to Sean with a kiss. He looks at her message, a heart with the words "Edwin loves Tony," and he gladly takes the bill and places it on the wall.

As they rejoin the group conversation, they hear Laci say, "That dress has been on the beach, to the Poconos, out and about in Chester County, at our house parties, but never ever has it been worn by a man, let alone in a drag show. This is like a dream come true! I love you, Danny!" She has ordered a tray of her favorite panty dropper shots plus two tequilas, and they all raise their glasses.

Jen is looking into her phone, walks over to Maggie, and shows her the initial results, 3,044 likes on Facebook, 5,432 shares, and Instagram is clicking away at 6,888. Maggie is about to check twitter when Becca shrieks, "Andy Cohen and Ellen DeGeneres have retweeted us!"

Jen proclaims, "We did it! Let the internet and millennials bring us home."

Maggie unlocks her phone to see a message from Patrick, which she promptly shows to the girls. The message contains a stream of rainbows and hearts with a message "So proud to call you my mother." A tear escapes Maggie's eye. Danny grabs her phone, clicks on the photo of Maggie's son, and says, "When do I get an introduction?"

"How about never," she responds, which causes Scott to laugh hysterically.

The drag show has resumed. Maggie sees Sean losing interest. She pulls him aside and says, "Hey, I have to stay, but you don't."

"Okay. Let me make some goodbyes first."

As Sean leaves her side, Larry hands her a very strong margarita. Her brother's friend is now next to her asking her how this came about. Maggie politely explains while keeping an eye on Sean. He is spending a few minutes with each of her friends, but when he comes to Laci, he leans in and says something that makes her climb over Danny to give Sean a nearly bare-chested monkey hug. He is smiling until he sees some yahoo bothering Maggie. Scott makes an attempt to speak to him, but Sean hears little of it. He is a dark cloud crossing an open vista.

He reaches Maggie, glares at the unknown man, and places his arm around her waist. She smiles and makes introductions. Tommy McGovern from Ardmore, Pennsylvania, takes the hint and buzzes off, but not before saying, "Can't wait to tell your brother I ran into you."

Maggie answers back, "Hey, Tommy." He turns, she smiles, eyes electric, and says, "Fuck off!" Tommy cracks up and walks away.

Sean asks, "Was that a term of endearment in your neighborhood, Maggie?"

"One might say it served a multitude of purposes."

Sean takes her by the hand and heads toward the door. Maggie quickly drinks the margarita as she walks with him. Jen and Emily watch, placing bets on whether or not she will be back. Cassie and Larry are dancing with the DC boys, and Laci is in deep conversation with Scott while still largely unclothed. Andrew has left his post at the door, allowing Maggie and Sean to slip outside unnoticed.

They both inhale the fresh cool air and begin to laugh at the absurdity of the last half hour. Sean looks to left and pulls her along until they cross the front of the building and yanks her into a small alley between the bar and a real estate office. He slides her up against the wall and kisses her until she stops him.

"Knock it off or I'm going to end up doing you right here."

"Well, that would be a first."

"That doesn't mean it's a good idea."

He leans in, speaking softly in her ear while brushing her cheek with his whiskers, and sighs, "All right, I'm walking up to get in my car and head home. The door will be unlocked. You need to celebrate with your friends. The five of you are a force." He leans back enough to look into her eyes in the dimly lit alley. "Tony would have loved it. He would have loved you."

In a rare moment of insecurity, he continues, "If you don't come by tonight, I'll take that as my answer."

Before Maggie can ask him the answer to what, he is kissing her again. Her mind swears she hears him say, "Don't go." This time Maggie pulls him into the streetlight so she can see him more clearly and says, "I'll see you after we wrap up here." She is feeling a little tipsy and asks, "What's the name of your street again?"

"Give me your hand." He reaches around to her back jeans pocket and takes the Sharpie she had used on the dollar bill and writes on her palm, "Please return to Oak Ave."

She giggles and says, "I'm gonna hate you for that in the morning."

He kisses her again, turns, and starts walking. She watches and wonders, what answer? How is she supposed to focus with him walking away, broad shoulders, long legs. *Aww, shit*, she warns herself, *do not check out his ass in those jeans. Sigh, too late.*

After he crosses Second Street, she turns to go inside and almost runs right into someone. "Oh, Scott, I'm sorry I almost knocked you over. Were you trying to catch him?"

"No, I'm trying to catch you." He hesitates before continuing, "Listen, Maggie, he's important to a lot of people here, and beyond important to people like Jim and me, who have seen him through a great deal."

She eyes him carefully as he continues, "Tell me you're not going to leave him in shreds."

An Uber pulls up, and Scott turns to get in it, but Maggie grabs his sleeve. "Just so you know, Scott, if there's going to be shreds left behind, some of them will belong to me."

With that, Maggie Burke is headed full stride back to the bar. She stops for a double tequila, neat, and heads back to her friends.

CHAPTER 19

Return to Sender

"Is that water?" Jen asks as she grabs the glass and sniffs. "Whoa, guess not. Come, Maggie, let's hit the dance floor."

"You go. I'll catch up." Jen eyes her carefully but decides to give her some space. Maggie starts playing with the Sharpies splayed across the table as she sips her tequila. A man stops by her table. "Looks like someone needs a friend," he offers.

Maggie lifts her head, looks him dead in the eyes, and says, "Keep moving before I hurt you."

"Nice attitude."

She seethes, "Are you still here?"

Jesse comes over to rescue her, pulling her onto the dance floor as Gaga sings "Bad Romance." Maggie is feeling the effects of the tequila and starts laughing at the irony of the song as she and Jesse join the others. Laci is flying high from panty droppers by now, moving across the dance floor to make certain all have experienced the Laci love. Maggie's brain registers this is usually when she starts to pull together an exit plan to get them home safely, but she knows she does not have it in her tonight.

A few songs later, she returns to their table. She bangs down the remaining tequila and reaches into her jeans for her cash. She separates the singles out. She has three. She grabs the red, black, and purple markers. On the first one, she writes in red, "Sean + Maggie = Hot." On the second, she writes in purple, "Sean + Maggie = ?" With the final bill, she opens the black pen and boldly writes, "Sean, I'm sorry."

Cassie sits down across from her, and Maggie pulls the bills close to her. Cassie asks, "Gonna leave your mark on this place, Maggie? Because I'm pretty sure we've already taken care of that."

Maggie smiles at her friend. "Yes, we did." Her smile fades, and she speaks from her heart to her, "Cassie, don't pursue Coach Turner unless you're sure. Because where I'm at right now just plain sucks."

Cassie waves to Emily to come over as Maggie fans out the dollars on the table. Message sides are facedown. Emily walks up to the table and asks, "What's up?"

Cassie explains, "I think the inevitable is about to happen. We're headed for a crash, like a head-on collision with reality crash."

Emily reaches toward the dollars. "What's this?" Maggie pulls the bills closer, and Emily continues, "Seriously, Maggie, I got your phone. Do you really think I'm not going to get my hands on those bills?"

Maggie starts to laugh and puts them down her blouse. Emily responds and says, "Nice. Cassie, go get the girls. The tequila is kicking in, and I'm not handling this alone." As Cassie moves to the dance floor, Emily sees the writing on Maggie's palm and thinks, *Damn right we are returning her.*

After several attempts, Laci comes off the dance floor when Jen gives her an exaggerated plea telling her Maggie really needs her. Laci is hugging Maggie all the way out the door. Emily and Cassie walk in front of the two of them, toting the wedding dress as Jen brings up the rear, a careful eye on the two inebriated women in front of her.

"Stop hugging me, I'm fine," giggles Maggie. She suddenly stops at the alley, swings Laci around to face it, and says, "He's a very bad boy. Do you know what he wanted to do in there?"

Laci lets loose a howl, "Yeah, I do! Why didn't you?" Together they start singing "Bad Romance."

Jen pushes them along and calls out to Cassie, "Back up, please!"

A very zigzagged two blocks later, they are close to Emily's SUV when they pass a cop just after Maggie and Laci sing, "I'm a free bitch, baby!" and Maggie calls out, "Hey, Officer, I think I need to file a complaint."

Jen grabs her and says, "For once in your life, shut up."

The cop walks over and says, "Hi, Maggie. Everything okay?"

"Hi. See, Jen, I know him." She sways a bit. "We met volunteering at the shelter this morning. We're fine…mostly. Just a little overserved. Do you know Sean?"

"I do." The cop is smiling.

"Well, he has messed with my head, and I don't like it."

The cop smiles, nods, and says, "Hmm, it happens." He turns to Jen and says, "You're going home, right?"

Emily walks over and says, "Yes, but we have one stop first." She grabs Maggie's hand, turns it over, and shows it to the officer.

He eyes Maggie and thinks of the woman he met this morning and the current mess in front of him. "Give the man what he asked for, serves him right." And with that, he hands Jen a card, "Call me if you need backup," and walks away.

Cassie piles Laci into the back seat of the Tahoe. She slides over and pats the seat, asking Maggie to be next to her. Cassie answers, "No problem."

Maggie climbs in next, and she says to Laci, "Guess where we're going?"

Emily asks the other women to get in the car quickly so she can get the child locks on. "Someone read the name of that street on Maggie's hand. It's a tree."

"Well, considering I'm the only fairly sober person back here, I think that's me," replies Cassie as Jen and Emily laugh. Cassie grabs Maggie's hand and asks for lights. She has grabbed the wrong hand.

Laci has the other and yells out, "It's palm tree, get it?" which causes Maggie and Laci to collapse in a fit of laughter. Cassie grabs the other hand and tells Emily the correct street name. She has buckled them both in and gives Emily the go ahead to move while telling the women up front that they officially owe her a babysitting fee.

As they turn onto Oak Avenue, Emily has no choice but to rely on Maggie to tell her which house. The car slowly rolls along as Maggie gazes out the window saying, "Not that one, not that one." They come to the beach path at the end of the street. Jen tells Emily to turn around and head up the street again, knowing her friend has only looked out of Laci's window.

Maggie is now counting houses. "Four, five, oh, that's Jim's house. Isn't he a sweetheart? He should give Sean some lessons on how to be nice." Emily is still slowly rolling, and she hears, "There it is! Let's go. I have a few things I need to tell him."

Emily nudges Jen, and they quickly get out of the vehicle while locking the doors. Jen comes around to Emily's side and asks, "What's next?"

Emily is about to explain her plan when she sees leopard heels being dropped in the front passenger seat and Maggie Burke climbing into the driver's seat. Before she can stop her, Maggie is honking the horn. Emily unlocks the door, turns to Jen, and says, "I think we're winging it."

As they head toward the porch steps, Maggie calls out, "Night, Jim," and the lights in front room of Sean's house go on, followed by porch lights. Maggie navigates the steps quickly and is about to knock on the front door when it opens. She has her hands on her hips, a determined look in her eyes. Sean smiles past her to her friends. "Big finish at the Parrot, I guess?"

Jen gently pushes Maggie forward, and Sean opens the screen door wider, "Sorry, I was asleep. Come in. Come in. Maggie, where are your shoes?"

Once inside, Maggie starts right in on him, "You were not asleep. You don't sleep in your jeans. As a matter of fact, girls, Sean sleeps in—"

Jen turns to her friend, takes the back of Maggie's head with her left hand while covering her mouth with her right, and says, "Normally your quick wit and biting tongue are two of your greatest assets, but not tonight, Maggie. So shut up!"

Maggie gives Jen a wounded look and nods her head yes. Emily steps up and addresses Sean, "We have a bit of a mess here, Sean. And from where we stand, you helped create a lot of it, so we'd like you to clean it up."

Maggie turns to go, saying, "I don't like this. I don't want to be here." She loses her balance, and Sean catches her. He nods to Jen. "Go, I've got her." Emily waits for a moment, watching as Maggie starts to eye the staircase.

Emily begins, "Look, Sean, this is new territory for her. She normally takes care of the rest of us when we go a little overboard. Here are a few things you need to know. One, she stops cursing when she drinks tequila. There is nothing wrong, just weird but true. Two, we have to get out of the rental house by ten. And three, do not leave her alone! At least not until you drop her safely with us."

Maggie steps back from Sean and says, "I changed my mind. We're going upstairs, mister."

Sean flatly says, "Yes, we are. Emily, run back to the kitchen and bring me the bottle of Advil by the faucet, will you?" Emily zips to get it and hands it to Sean as she keeps moving toward the front door.

She turns around, smiles at Sean, and says, "Good luck."

Maggie answers, "Yeah, because he's gonna need it."

Sean shoves the Advil in his pocket, steers Maggie to the steps, smiles at Emily, and says, "Yes, I am. Night, Em."

Rosie is laying on the floor by Sean's side of the bed and lifts her head as Sean and Maggie enter the room. Sean thinks, *Thanks a bunch, girl.* He can feel Maggie crashing with each step and begins to talk to her. "Let's get you into bed. You're going to let me help you." He kisses the top of her head as he gets her by the bed.

Tears are fighting to stay in her eyes, and he calms her, "There's nothing to cry about, Maggie. It's all going to be okay." He encourages her to get her jeans off as he heads to the bathroom for water and the flannel shirt she has made her own. He returns handing her the water and three Advils. "Drink the whole glass, Maggie." She does, and as he bends to pick up her jeans, she floats three single-dollar bills to the floor.

She giggles. "I just wanted to see you bend over again." He cannot help but laugh at her. She is totally ridiculous.

She hands him the water glass, and he places it and the bills on his nightstand while tossing her jeans to a waiting chair. He hears her softly speak, "I wanted to tell you something, but I can't remember what it was."

"Then it's not important right now." He lifts her T-shirt over her head and hands her his flannel shirt.

She does her best to button up the shirt and says to herself, "That's what my dad used to say." He pulls down the covers, and she climbs in as he grabs the water glass and returns it to the bathroom. When he walks back into the bedroom, he notices that he knocked two of the dollar bills on the floor. She has her eyes closed and is close to falling asleep. He quietly picks up the bills and ends up reading all three before putting them in the front pocket of her jeans.

He considers sleeping in the guest room to not to disturb her but heeds Emily's warning instead as he disrobes and slides in next to her. He pulls her to him and softly says, "Maggie Burke, you are one hot, beautiful mess. God help me, I love you."

Somewhere in the recesses of her mind, it registers, and Maggie hugs him just a little tighter in her sleep.

CHAPTER 20

Gas Station Realization

Maggie senses light trying to infiltrate her eyelids and feels resentful. She rolls to her right and feels nothing. While the space is vacant, it's not cold either. She is in Sean's bed. She knows this because she now recognizes the smell of cedar from the box near his nightstand where he keeps stuff. She inhales again and identifies his brand of laundry detergent, Meyer's Lemon Verbena. She feels weight on her feet, which makes her smile—Rosie.

Before her brain can fully awaken, the bathroom door opens, steam escaping with it. She rolls in that direction and slowly opens her eyes to see Sean standing there, wet hair and towel around his hips. She thinks God must be punishing her to put that sight in front of her right now.

"Good morning. How are you feeling?" he asks.

She struggles to pull herself up with a small groan. "A little shaken up and definitely sad." She puts a hand to her forehead and says, "Could be worse. I think you took care of me last night. Thank you."

"Well, it took a village, but yes, you obviously ended up here. I did what I could."

"Oh Lord, I'm a hot mess." Suddenly Maggie pauses as a faint memory tries to jog itself loose in her brain. Sean walks into his closet and puts on a pair of jeans and a T-shirt. Her inner voice asks her, *Why can men do that? They don't care who sees their ass.* She answers herself, *Because theirs holds up a lot better than ours, that's why.*

Sean vigorously towel dries his hair, tosses the towel in a hamper, and emerges from his closet putting some kind of product in his hair. He walks over, gives Rosie the move-over sign, and sits by her feet. Maggie begins to curl her knees up to her chest in just enough time to bury her head there while he speaks.

"It's past seven thirty. You need to get up, shower, and pull yourself together. You have to be out of your rental by ten."

Without lifting her head, Sean clearly hears her response, "Goddamn it, it's Monday."

He thinks to himself, *I guess the tequila is out of her system*, and continues, "I think you know where everything is. Get moving."

She swings her feet out of bed and pauses. "Wait, are you actually mad at me?"

He stands, pulls her to her feet, and calmly says, "No, but for the first time, I'll be the one to say this. We have run out of time. No tears. Let's just put one foot in front of the other, okay?"

With that, he walks out of the room asking, "Coffee or Coke?"

"A Coke please." Maggie heads to the shower, where she has herself a good cry whether he likes it or not.

Maggie is about to put on her clothes from last night for the third consecutive morning but goes into his closet to grab a clean T-shirt. One from the Born in the USA Tour jumps out at her, so she puts it on over her jeans. She thinks she must have left her shoes downstairs, so she gathers up what is hers without making the bed and descends the staircase.

She walks toward the kitchen, and Sean sees a bewildered look on her face as he pours the Coke. "Nice shirt. Am I going to get it back?"

There is no sparring, no direct answer. Instead, she asks, "Have you seen my shoes?"

"Nope. You waltzed in here barefoot last night." Sean is channeling Jim's advice but finding it horribly difficult to not swoop in and fix this for her.

Maggie is sipping her Coke and slowly puts it down, eyes widening a bit as the memory of tossing her heels in the front of

Emily's car comes to her, and she groans, "Why, why did I drink tequila all night?"

"Yeah, I'd take it off my short list if I were you."

That remark earns him the first sign of lightning bolts to come from her eyes, and he thinks, *There we go, Maggie, let's get some sparks flying from that brain of yours.* Although she is still not up to sparring, she fires one back, "Well, that bartender at the Parrot didn't help. She has a thing for you, Sean, be careful."

"Noted" is all he offers as he grabs his keys out of the pewter dish and walks toward the garage, leaving her to finish her drink. He has pulled the Jeep out onto the street to warm up. He comes through the kitchen, sees Maggie on a barstool, and flatly informs her, "We gotta go."

Maggie stoops down to give Rosie a hug and says, "At least you still love me," which elicits a very firm "Don't" from Sean. Maggie follows him out the front door, down the steps, and thinks, *Yeah right, you are not pissed at all.* As they pull away, she regrets that she will not get to say goodbye to Jim.

The ride to the beach rental is quiet, too quiet. Maggie's anxiety is rearing, but so is her temper. As they pass the hotels on Boardwalk Avenue, Sean finally speaks, "Look, I want to help you girls load your cars and then make our goodbyes. Apparently, you need space to sort through whatever is keeping you from getting to the same place I am. So let's just talk in a few days…and hopefully you can give me some kind of an answer by then."

Maggie is genuinely confused, and feeling the pressure of being blocks away from the house, she blurts out, "Answer to what exactly?"

Sean cannot help himself. For a man who prides himself on not losing his temper, he is exasperated. He pulls the Jeep over to the curb, looks at her, and blasts, "Are you freaking kidding me, Maggie?"

"No, I'm not. There are too many unanswered questions, Sean. How am I supposed to know which one?" She reaches up to touch the top of her banging head.

"Damn it, woman, figure it out. And then call me." He puts the Jeep in gear and goes forty-five in a twenty-five. They are in front of the house in three minutes. There is no way she is waiting for him to get her door. She is out with a slam, marching toward the house. He remains in the Jeep, his head bent and thinking, *You had better be right, Jim*, when Emily taps on his window. He opens his door and gets out.

She gives him a hug and asks, "Not all cleaned up yet, is it? Come on, give me a hand with the back of the Tahoe."

Sean starts pulling out everything per Emily's instructions while she folds, consolidates, and packs. Together they start lining up things to go back versus trash from the lower level, upper deck, and hot tub area. All the while Emily is coaching.

"You're doing great, Sean. Stay in it, but don't do the work for her. She has shut herself off from a relationship for years in order to survive raising those kids while Kevin did whatever he wanted. She handled everything, even their divorce, with little to no drama. And then you come along…and she's made herself a total mess, when it's really pretty simple."

"How simple, Emily?"

"You are into her…big-time. She is into you…also big-time. So…date."

"Thanks, Em, I agree, but for a few minutes there, I thought I was losing my mind."

Emily laughs and says, "That's ironic because that's what she told me about you on Friday night."

They stand back and look at the reorganized, partially loaded Tahoe, and Sean says, "You know, Emily, you have the makings of a really good roadie."

She responds with a smile and gives him a hug and says, "Roadie, soccer mom, it's all the same thing."

One by one, the women's suitcases and laundry baskets come down for Emily and Sean to load. Jen brings a half-full case of champagne, which Sean promptly takes from her as she uses Maggie's car keys to pop the trunk of the Audi. He laughs and says, "You really don't ever run out of champagne, do you?"

Jen smiles and asks, "Never. Do you think she should drive home? She's barely talking."

Sean answers, "She needs a chocolate milkshake and a cheeseburger stat, but if you can drive stick, you should." Jen nods in agreement.

Cassie brings down Maggie's assorted kitchen supplies, which Sean takes from her and places in the trunk. He asks Cassie if Maggie is making any progress, and she gives him the so-so sign. He frowns and heads inside, to which Cassie simply says, "Yikes."

Laci hits him up at the top of the stairs with her garment bag and Emily's craft toolbox. He can't help but laugh at the sight of her as the silver hair seems to be a permanent treatment, not a wig. He chuckles and says to her, "Laci, you got some 'splaining to do when you get home."

She, too, is laughing and says, "My kids have come to expect it, and my husband will use it to his advantage, if you know what I mean."

As they return inside for another trip, Laci stops him for a moment. "Sean, thank you for telling me about your brother last night. I'm so glad I got to see a glimpse of him through you." Sean hugs her again, and she whispers, "And as for that one upstairs...go get her, Sean."

He replies, "Nope, she's got to come to me, Laci. I have been chasing her for four days, and while I do not regret a minute of it, it's on her now. And you can't help either."

Laci allows Sean to go up alone. He finds Maggie sitting on the bed she should have slept in, linens folded in a laundry basket, duffel bag, computer bag, and purse are packed and ready. She is combing through her phone, looking back through their text messages, trying to figure out the question for which he wants an answer. She looks up at him, eyes searching blankly.

"You won't find it in your phone, Maggie. Let it go. It will come to you." He pulls her to her feet and embraces her for what feels like a very long time and yet not long enough before saying, "Time to head out."

"Wait," she chokes before putting her arms around his neck and kissing him goodbye. No other words come to her, her mind cluttered, her heart heavy.

Cassie and Laci sit in the car. Laci is in the passenger seat crying for her friend as Cassie hands her tissues trying not to laugh at the ridiculousness of the silver hair. Emily and Jen are standing behind the Audi, waiting for them to come out, when Jen turns her back and says, "This is going to be brutal. I can't look."

Emily says, "That's okay, you've got the toughest job. You have to get her home."

Jen remembers his instructions. "He wants us to get some fast food into her."

"There's a Wendy's next to a gas station on the Coastal Highway heading out. We will stop there. If she's too depressed by then, Cassie is going with you, and I'm sticking Laci on her ass."

Maggie exits first, Athletica pants, black quarter zip, Phillies baseball cap pulled low, and sunglasses on. Sean locks the door and drops the keys in the lockbox, turning the lock. He picks up her things and brings them to the Audi. She walks over and snaps, "Seriously, Jen, why is the roof not down?" Emily smiles at Sean as if to say that's a good sign before they all get in their cars and pull away.

Jen turns the audio on to hear Springsteen's voice, and Maggie dives for the power button. "If that man has ruined The Boss for me, I will never forgive him."

Jen offers, "Mags, put your seat back. You've had a rough night."

Maggie agrees. Sleep might be in order. It sure as hell beats the reality of the situation. Twenty minutes later, Jen pulls the Audi into the gas station and asks, "Premium in this bad boy?"

Maggie reaches for her wallet. and Jen continues, "Knock it off, put that away. You drove down. I'll cover the gas going home."

Maggie peers in the direction of the mini-mart of the gas station and gets out of the car. She hears Cassie and Laci say they are going to Wendy's and ask for her order. She waves them off. The women look at each other, and Jen instructs, "Just get her a cheeseburger. She's going for Smart Water."

Maggie aimlessly wanders the aisles, ends by the drinks, and pulls five bottles of Smart Water from the refrigerator shelves. She juggles them as she walks up to the counter and sees the lottery display. She slowly places the water on the counter and asks for five

Powerball tickets. The man behind the counter takes a good look at her, noticing that she looks distracted. Maggie pulls two twenties and the singles out of her jeans. She rereads the Sharpie messages on each bill as the man behind the counter asks, "Is there something more, miss?"

Maggie's mind clicks on a memory from Friday night.

"First of all, I haven't been active in way too long. You want to do a medical check on me, ask the drummer, he's my doc. Secondly, what you, or shall I say we, are trying to do is figure out if this is a, a harmless flirtation, it's not, b, a magnetically charged sexual attraction, it is, and c, if there is any shot at creating something more in the next forty-eight hours, personally I'd like to know."

She snaps her head up. "Oh my god, that's it!" The man prints out the lottery tickets and hands them to her. She asks, "Is forty dollars enough?" He answers that it's too much as she grabs the singles, frantically scoops up the bottles of water and the lottery tickets, and races out the door like a bat out of hell.

CHAPTER 21

Scene of the Crime

"Jen, get in the car, quick! I have to go back."

Emily looks at Jen. "Did she just rob a convenience store? I'm out if she did."

Jen takes the bottles from Maggie. "You paid for these, right?" Then she eyes the lottery tickets. "And these, you didn't, like, beat up a nun for this stuff, did you, Maggie?"

"Oh, shut up, let's go. Actually, I'll drive."

"Maggie, Emily's gas guzzler is still fueling. Calm down and tell me what's going on, and maybe by then frick and frack will have returned. And you're not driving because I'm not entirely sure you're sober."

"Screw you, Jen, it's my car."

"Okay, you're probably sober, but I'm still driving. That way you can tell me what the hell is going on while we go wherever the hell you need to go to in such a hurry."

Laci strolls over midcheeseburger and asks, "Something is going on. What? Is it Maggie? Danny? Sean? What? I need to know!"

"So we've crossed over to the asylum check in phase, I see," says Cassie.

Maggie is literally pushing the women toward their designated cars. She tells them she will call from her car, to put her on Bluetooth, and it will all make sense. She notices the time and tries to make her best guess at where Sean would be at ten thirty-five on a Monday morning.

As the mini caravan heads south on the coastal highway. Maggie punches in Emily is number and is connected. Laci is beside herself. "Girl, what gives?"

"We are going back to Sean's house. You all have to listen to me on this. I finally figured it out."

Jen interrupts, "We know that much already."

"Shut up and drive, Jen," snaps Maggie. "All this time he's been waiting for me to tell him this is something more than just a fling. I swear, he is kind of an idiot. Who does that shit?"

Jen says, "At the risk of you going for my throat here, are you sure he isn't the only idiot in this relationship? We all could have told you this."

"Then why didn't you?"

Emily answers from her car, "Because you needed to figure it out for yourself. So now what, Maggie?"

Maggie excitedly says, "Jen, go left, now!"

Jen whips to left by the outlets, Emily close behind her. "Mags, where are we going? This isn't town."

"Turn left in that parking lot and pull up by that entrance." As Jen stops the car, Maggie is out like a shot, barreling through the double doors. The women stare at the doorway and see the Tony DeMarco Home for Men.

Emily acknowledges it first. "Wow, he built this? I thought she was volunteering at a government shelter."

Cassie says, "I think Sean must be loaded. Who knew?"

Jen knows her best friend and answers, "I'm thinking she did. It would definitely add to her anxiety."

Maggie comes running out, jumps in the Audi, and says, "Keep going, he's not there." As Jen pulls out, Emily is honking and yelling through the phone, "Wait! Wait! Danny is running out of the shelter. Maggie, what the hell?"

Danny opens the back door of Emily's car and jumps in next to Laci. "Sorry, I've got skin in the game too... Go, go!" Laci brings Danny up to speed explaining that they are heading to Sean's house. He tells them he knows a shortcut to get there.

As they enter the circle, Danny yells, "Take the circle all the way around, Jen, then go right on Columbia."

She follows Columbia, and Danny instructs her to take a right on Second Avenue. "Oh, I've got it, there's Oak." Jen zips down Oak, with Emily right behind her. They cross over first, and Jen says to Maggie, "Which one? It was so dark last night."

Cassie deadpans, "Don't you mean this morning?"

"Right there, Jen, the big porch. Just park at the curb."

Jen puts the car in park and asks, "Now what?"

"I'm going in, that's what." Maggie rockets out of her car.

Everyone gets out of the cars to form a huddle near the Tahoe. Cassie asks, "Does anyone else think she's losing it? I feel very OJ and the LAPD right now."

Jen replies, "Oh great, that makes me Al Cowlings."

Maggie tries the front door—locked. She knocks and peers through the front living room window. Rosie is barking at her. "I know, girl, I'm sorry, but your dad's an idiot. We'll straighten him out yet." She walks over to the garage and tries the right bay. The door goes up with no hesitation. She turns and waves her friends in.

"Okay, he's not here, but Rosie and the Jeep are. There are only two places left, Darby's or out on the bike. You all have lives waiting for you. I need you to leave me here. Jen, can you drive my car back?"

"That's insane, no."

"If I have it, there's a chance I'll run."

Laci chimes in, "She's right."

"Who can take Wilson? My poor boy, he's going to be so mad at me."

"I've got him," volunteers Emily. "He'll be fine. You are coming home at some point, right?"

"Danny, can you bring me my duffel bag, purse, and computer bag from the Audi?" Cassie goes with him to help identify the pieces.

They are all clustered in the garage as she explains that the laundry room door is probably open and she is going in to leave him a note should he come back. She will leave her things in his house. After that, she is walking to Darby's to wait for him. Laci has that look in her eye, and Maggie cuts her off at the pass, "No, you are not going in. That is considered breaking and entry. At least I have the excuse that I have slept with him for three consecutive nights. Now, get going before I change my mind."

Emily asks again, "Maggie, when are you coming home?"

"I'll be home by Friday at the latest."

The women are openmouthed and speechless. Maggie's eye sparkle as she laughs and says, "Just kidding. I'll be home tomorrow... evening-ish."

"How are you getting home?"

"Oh puhleeze, Sean's bringing me home. I am not worried about that. After all, I can be very persuasive. Besides, he kind of owes me for driving me completely insane!"

Laci and Danny say in unison, "Go get him, girl!"

They walk out of the garage as she enters the house, and they quickly huddle by the Tahoe. Jen starts, "We're not leaving Rehoboth yet, right?"

Emily is thinking, "Maybe we should. Look, he's crazy about her. I took a good look at him when he got back in his Jeep to leave this morning, not great, that's for sure."

Out of nowhere, Jim appears, "Ladies, hit the road. This is between the two of them."

Laci goes over to give him a hug and says, "I agree."

Jim responds, "Honey, what did they do to your hair?"

They decide to put their trust in Jim, but not before all enter his number in their phones and give him a kiss goodbye. He says, "Girls, I'm going to be seeing more of you. He understands she's a bit of a package deal. He needs more women in his life anyway."

"I knew it," exclaims Emily as she unlocks the doors and Danny and Laci climb in. Cassie and Jen get into the Audi and Jen receives a text.

"Thx, I O U."

Cassie turns to Jen and says, "Another epic adventure, that's for sure."

"Yeah, Mike's not going to believe it. Let's call him after we get on 95. I don't think I can wait until I get back to fill him in."

*****

Maggie has written Sean a note and left it on the kitchen counter by his pewter dish. On it she writes, "I remember what I wanted to tell you. Meet me at Darby's." She simply signs it "M." She runs upstairs to make the bed, but he has already come back to do it. She spies the flannel shirt draped on her side of the bed, a very sentimental act from a too-tidy man. She asks Rosie, "I did soften his hide, didn't I?"

With that, she heads back downstairs, pulls her makeup bag out, and hits the powder room to freshen up without overdoing it. She thinks she has about a ten- to twelve-block walk, just enough time to put her thoughts together and expend a little nervous energy. She mists her face and hair with rosewater, pulls a ponytail through her baseball cap, grabs her sunglasses, pats Rosie on the head, and says, "I'll be back."

She exits through the garage, pulling the door back down, when she hears, "Well, hello Maggie!"

She smiles at Jim and walks over to him. "Hi, Jim, I'm sorry, I can't talk right now. I have to find Sean and tell him something."

"I'm sure he's a work, dear. Let him have it, sweetie."

"That's the plan, Jim, that's the plan." She takes a few steps toward the street calls back to him, "Hey, Jim...looks like I've met someone who can give me a run for my money after all." She turns toward First Avenue, but not before catching a thumbs-up from Jim.

Maggie sets out, lifting her face to the autumn sun. She decides to take First Avenue over to Rehoboth Avenue and then go right until she hits Darby's. She's about five blocks in when a cop car slows, sliding the window down. She lifts her sunglasses and looks in. The cop calls out, "Hi, Maggie! All good with that complaint of yours?"

She must be feeling better because she remembers the conversation from last night walks over to his car and says, "I'm so sorry about last night. I am blaming it on the tequila. As for the complaint, he's about to get an earful." The officer gives her a smile with a nod and drives on. People are walking their dogs, the mail carrier walks his route, and all are saying, "Hey, Maggie, great job last night."

She thinks the bar must have been more crowded than she realized. She continues pulling her thoughts together as she goes along. She makes a right onto Rehoboth Avenue. She passes one beautiful storefront after another, and several proprietors wave to her. She is curious until she sees a newspaper box and the headline, "PA Women Send Message to Supreme Court," below it a picture of the five of them with the banner. She digs for quarters and finds enough to take one paper. She will stop and get more before she heads home. Then it registers, she does not have her car. *Keep walking*, she tells herself, and she tosses the paper in her bag.

Another ten minutes goes by, she finds herself across the street from Darby's. She studies the entrance and makes some mental notes. He needs to purchase the lot behind it in order to provide more parking, big potted flowers for spring, and an elaborate multicolored light display in honor of Tony and Edwin for Christmas. Maggie crosses the street and walks toward the rear entrance, no Harley. *Just as well*, she thinks. She checks her phone, 11:40. She walks back to the entrance and opens the door.

*****

Sean has run the bike through Ocean City, Maryland, and back trying to clear his head to no avail. He swings up Boardwalk Avenue, passes the rental house, and thinks about her in the kitchen. He parks by the beach path, walks to the crest of it, and looks out at the ocean. No mermaid in sight. He pauses and wonders how close to home she might be by now. Back on the bike, he cruises up to Rehoboth Avenue, passes the Purple Parrot, and turns his head to look down the alley. He cannot believe that was less than twelve hours ago.

Van Morrison's "Celtic New Year" is playing through his helmet, and he considers stopping home to call her, but tells himself not just yet. He has to be patient and trust she knows him well enough by now to know what it is that he needs from her. The question is, what if she doesn't?

The melody and lyrics remind him of them as he rides through a few back streets. In the song, the man is clearly asking his woman to come back to him, but you never know if she does. He pulls into his spot behind Darby's clouded in melancholy. He looks at his phone, no message, no missed call. It's twelve eighteen. He assumes Monday regulars are at the bar and in for lunch. He heads into work intent on burying himself in some neglected paperwork.

*****

Forty minutes earlier, the front door opens, and Jesse greets the patron walking in. "Maggie, is that you?"

She removes her sunglasses. "I'm afraid so, Jesse. The Irish would say that I am like a bad penny. I keep turning up. Sorry about last night. I let the tequila and the night get away from me. Can I have some water, Jesse? I just walked from Sean's house, a beautiful day for it, but I'm parched."

"First of all, you are not a bad penny." He slaps the article in front of her as he squeezes some lemon into her water, sliding it her way. He leans over and points to the number of times Maggie, Becca, and Darby's are mentioned in print. She sees her name and gives him a quizzical look. "Maggie, it was your personal Twitter feed. You were the easiest to identify. Nice LinkedIn by the way. Sorry, but you've gone viral."

"Geez, well, if it helps the Supreme Court get it done, then great."

Suddenly Becca is at the service bar. "Maggie?"

Maggie grabs her water and walks to Becca. "Your boss in by any chance?"

"Not yet, but he should be here in about fifteen minutes. Can I get you anything?" She looks at Jesse, who shrugs and puts his hands up.

"No, I'm fine. Actually, do you mind if I walk around a bit? I'm not great standing still."

"No problem. I'll leave the office unlocked if you'd like to wait for him in there."

Maggie smiles. "No way, I almost killed him in there Friday night."

Becca laughs. "You know why? Because it is claustrophobic in there. I've been asking him to either put in a window or blow it out somehow."

Maggie's brow furrows. "And he hasn't listened to you?"

Becca tries to understand her confusion, or is it disappointment? "Maggie, he can be difficult to approach with new ideas. He's very accustomed to doing things his way because he built this business on his own."

"Becca, seriously, do you think I don't recognize a tight ass when I see one? He needs to be a little less predictable with his life before it's too late."

Becca smiles knowingly, testing her, "Should I call him and tell him you're here?"

"Nope, I'll wait." She thinks Sean's loss of his controlled environment and dependence on the predictable begins when it becomes his turn to receive a surprise by what he finds in his place of business. She walks out to the terrace, heads directly to the fountain, and says a little prayer to Edwin and Tony. She needs a little Divine intervention today. The fountain calms her racing mind. She scans the terrace for a better location for it, and as she turns, she looks at the wall and for the first time is glad she did not scale it that night.

Jesse has Springsteen playing through the restaurant as she reenters from the garden. She hears "Waiting on a Sunny Day." She walks over places her water glass down, shakes her head, and tells him, "You are shameless."

Jesse smiles at her as he says, "Sean needs all the help he can get. I'm pulling for you guys."

Becca now joins them. "Honestly, Maggie. He's been kind of stuck for a couple of years." She observes these young protégées understand him more than he realizes. Becca continues, "He needs you to keep pushing him out of his comfort zone."

Maggie considers that statement and heads into the dining room with the stage as Clarence Clemens soulfully carries the melody with his sax over the sound system. She sees Sean's Gibson in a stand. She thinks, *Good grief, man, put your toys away.* Suddenly she understands why he is so orderly at home but not so much here. He is working too much, she should know.

She drifts back to the table in the corner where she and her friends sat Friday night. She puts down her purse with the newspaper in it. She watches Becca handle the lunch regulars in the other room, and then she hears the rumble of a Harley engine. She smiles with the knowledge of being one step ahead of Sean DeMarco.

Jesse pours her another water and waves her in. She walks toward him, and he tells her to stand to the left of the service bar. "Trust me, he stops there first when he comes in." She shakes her head no, takes the water and a cocktail napkin, deposits them at the table as well, and heads back to the stage. She had noticed six tables filled in the dining room and about five men at the bar. She thinks he should close Monday through Wednesday in the off-season, just bring managers in for paperwork and marketing efforts as needed. She adds that to her mental list of things to talk to him about.

Becca is now standing at the service bar. Maggie hears her say, "Hi, Sean, did you know you had an appointment?"

Maggie sees Becca out of the corner of her eye, pointing in the direction of the stage. Bruce is now singing "I'm Going Down." The beat of the song helps her to focus. Maggie turns so that her back is fully to the bar, steeling herself for what she is about to say. She hears his steps and remains perfectly still until she hears him address her.

"Maggie?"

She slowly turns around to face him. No daggers, no tears. He tries to get a read on her but cannot. He takes a step closer. "What are you doing here?"

Still nothing. He takes another step and tries again, "You want to give me a clue?"

There it is. She knew she just had to wait for it. She raises her eyebrow just a bit. "I think you need to buy a few clues, Sean. Let's start with your business."

She eyes Becca at the table behind Sean, walks over between them, arms crossed in front of her, and says, "You need to get your artistic head out of your ass." She points to Becca. "Do you know what you have here? I worked alongside her last night, she's very sharp. She has great ideas, and you are ignoring her. Do you want to lose her? Because you will."

He waits, because he knows more is coming. "And another thing, fire that bookkeeper. She is lazy. It's lunchtime on a Monday after a record-breaking Friday, and she's not here yet."

Becca adds, "She's right, Sean."

He shoots Becca a look that causes her to freeze on the spot, incapable of speaking or moving.

He turns his attention back to Maggie. "Anything else?"

Maggie's tone softens, "Yes, you need to change the lighting by the fountain. It is beautiful, fluid, and calming, and people need to see it better. Actually, you should move it to the center of your courtyard."

Becca feels like she is watching a car wreck in slow motion. She quietly steps away from her table but remains close enough to listen.

He sighs, "Nothing else?"

"One more thing, can you give me a ride home?" She pauses and lets it sink in before she adds, "Tomorrow."

He walks to her, pulls off the baseball cap, and says, "I will need an answer to my question."

"Well, I have your answer, but you really could have given me a few clues when I was confused."

"You're right. I'm sorry."

Her eyes are wide, her head tilted, and she knows she has him in the palm of her hand. "Ask me again, Sean, please."

The dark eyes are now warm as he asks, "Is this something more?"

She kisses him first and then gives him her allusive one-word answer, "Yes."

CHAPTER 22

Emily

Emily and Laci offer hugs goodbye to Danny in front of the Tony DeMarco Home for Men with a promise to stay in touch. Emily checks the back of the Tahoe and with all in good order begins the trek back to Chester County. The women share a twenty-minute recap of their finale to this year's vacation with Laci giving the growing stats on their social media campaign.

"Em, I think these numbers are huge. I cannot wait to hear what Jen thinks when she gets home later today. You know she'll be checking them. That girl loves the data."

Emily eases onto Route 113 N adding, "It was so smart to get Patrick on board. I think the twenty-somethings made the difference. I bet Maggie and Jen brainstormed the whole time they were getting dressed to go out. Kept someone's mind off the inevitable goodbye until this morning."

Laci stares out the window. "Do you think she'll be home tonight or tomorrow? He seemed pretty resigned that it was over when he was helping me move my stuff."

The next half hour is a recap of the lightening in a bottle that was Maggie's romance in Rehoboth, ending with Emily saying, "It's far from over, Laci. I have been watching him since he laid eyes on her. He has fallen for her big-time. I do believe she has too, but way behind him in realizing it...and that is okay. Whatever it turns out to be, it's great seeing her like this."

By the time Emily helps Laci unload her supplies, props, and essentials, their phones have a ridiculous amount of activity in the form of text messages, missed calls, and social media alerts. Dex emerges from the garage, takes one look at his wife's hair, and starts grinning. "The internet does not do it justice." He reaches out touches it, kisses his wife, and says, "Kind of kinky. I think I like it."

Laci offers, "Wait till you see the costume that goes with it."

Emily shuts her cargo area, gives a quick hug goodbye, and says, "Why do I think Dex has those kids down for a nap already?"

"You're damn right I do."

Moments later, Emily pulls her car into her driveway after dropping Laci and her trunk show of garments at home. A quick group text from Maggie came across about ten minutes earlier saying "All good here" and nothing more. She is dying for details but knows she will have Wilson, which means she is the most likely to get them first. She turns off her ignition to see JT coming out of the house, Bluetooth affixed to his ear, and ready to empty the Tahoe for her. The dogs beat a path in her direction, wagging and circling her in an official welcome home.

"I've got corporate on mute." He gives her a kiss and a squeeze and says, "We missed you, sweetie. A good trip?"

"Always is. Did you go on social media at all?"

JT looks at her as if she has two heads and laughs. She responds, "This can wait. Let's talks when your call ends."

They grab her laundry basket and duffel bag and head into the mudroom so she can start to put her wash, house, and family back on track after four days away. There are updates on the girls and their soccer games and social activities but mostly it is the lunch from Wegman's that's waiting for her that reminds her what a keeper her guy is and how much she loves her life.

After they have eaten and cleaned up, Emily gives a high-level explanation of what has happened with Maggie. She asks JT to go over to Maggie's with her to pick up Wilson. He says, "Ya know, I always knew we'd end up taking care of someone's kids or animals after one of these trips, but I never guessed it would be Maggie's. You girls are really okay with all of this?"

"Totally. I have a feeling you will meet him sooner than later. And, JT, he's the exact opposite of Kevin. I saw him notice her the minute he joined our group on the beach. He got a pen out and wrote something down on the back of a receipt. Next thing I know, he's handing it to her saying 'Text me.'"

JT grins at his wife. "And she didn't bitch-slap him?"

"If you want to hear it, I'll tell you the detailed story after the girls go to bed. Right now I just want to pick up her dog, get home, and let them all have a good run outside."

He grabs her keys and her hand and walks her out to the Tahoe. It takes them less than five minutes to arrive at Maggie's. Wilson is in the window barking as JT takes the key from under the dome of the garage carriage lamp. Wilson is out like a shot, and JT pulls the treat from his pocket to bring him back and says, "Come on, boy, your momma done abandoned you. But we've got your back until she gets her sinful ass home tomorrow."

Before they head into her house, Emily gives him a sassy kiss and says, "You know I love it when you let your country boy show."

Emily heads to the pantry closet in the kitchen to get Wilson's leash, a baggie full of his kibble, and a toy. JT is in Maggie's dining room with Wilson, and Emily asks, "What are you snooping around about?"

"Em, you might want to come here and look at this. She's putting the house on the market."

"Already?"

"From what I can tell, right after Christmas. Her kids are gonna bum."

"JT, stop reading that contract! It's none of our business." Still, Emily is not entirely surprised. This has all been three years in the making. "Maggie's job is here, she's just downsizing."

"She should or those kids will be moving back in. Let's remember that in ten to fifteen years, okay?"

Emily's phone rings, and she looks at it to see Jen's name. "Hey, I'm just picking up Wilson. What's up?"

After a series of "Yups," "Mmm-hmms," and one "Oh my god," Emily finally forms a full sentence, "Well, you'd better call her. She's the one with the most exposure after all."

She hangs up and begins to tell JT the latest. She kneels by Wilson and says, "Your momma's not just a tramp. She and Aunt Laci are a social media sensation. She's gotten us all our fifteen minutes of fame with her Twitter prowess." Wilson gives her a kiss while she attaches the lead as she and JT head home in time to greet their girls coming off the school bus.

CHAPTER 23

Jen

Mike hands Jen a fresh cup of coffee and watches her as she pops up her laptop, firing off an email to Bill Anderson at *Fox News* to offer times for the interview tomorrow. He tries to offer a suggestion, "Don't you think you should check to see if Maggie will be back by at least one of the times you are suggesting?"

"She'll be here. I'm ready to choke her right now because she hasn't given me a straight answer, but she owes the four of us, and I'm not afraid to play that card." Jen got the email from a *Fox News* producer before four o'clock asking for their group of friends to participate in an interview tomorrow about the viral social media campaign that went out Sunday night.

After gathering a few facts, the producer asked that they figure out one point person to handle the majority of the questions and the others be there to add color or details as necessary. Given the fact that Maggie had filmed numerous times for work, and had not bothered to come home with them, they all decided she was officially elected to the job. She attaches Maggie's bio from the nonprofit website and sends the email.

"Call her, Jen, before I do," threatens Mike.

*****

It is six thirty. Maggie and Sean are hanging by the fire she thought she would never see lit and watching CBS's *World News Report* when her phone rings. She smiles devilishly at Sean and

172

answers, "Well, hello there. I have not heard from you for at least an hour. What's up?"

"What are you doing right now?"

"Watching the news and waiting for the buzzer to go off on my chicken parm. Titillating, isn't it? Why?"

"Because I need you to pick a time for the interview tomorrow. Look, you are pissing me off. Just play nice. We have all been super supportive to you. We need you. You won't even flinch in front of the camera."

"First of all, there's rarely a camera anymore. They do all this shit with their phones unless it is a big story, which we are not. Secondly, I will be there as long as it is not before noon. I would really like to sleep in since I pretty much blew that opportunity over the past four days. What are you wearing for this?"

"Maggie, time, give me a solid time for the interview!"

"Geez, how's two? And I'm going to be in jeans and a blazer. I'll need to stop by my house, and then we'll be there."

"We?"

"Yup, my driver is probably staying over tomorrow night, but I hadn't asked him yet." Maggie gives Sean a smile before continuing, "Oops, there goes my timer. Gotta go, ttyl!"

*****

"Maggie, wait—" Jen turns to Mike and says, "She's much easier to deal with when she's not getting laid."

Mike gives her his most wicked look and says, "And you are much easier when you are. Let's go, wifey. We got some catching up to do."

By late the next morning, Jen has her kitchen set up as command central. Maggie sent her a press release around ten last night without a request from Jen. That went a long way to calming Jen's frayed nerves. She had forgotten how effortlessly they used to work together. She wonders why her friend works so hard for so little money and puts up with so much stress. She considers the possibility of them teaming up again as consultants and realizes Maggie's whole life is in change mode, so why not.

Emily and Laci are the first to arrive a little before one, anxious to hear what Jen has heard from Maggie. Before they can ask, Jen reports on an update, "*Fox News* is coming out before two. I checked Twitter today, and Maggie's original tweet with the photo has over two hundred thousand retweets."

Maggie enters from the mudroom. "It was that great photo, buddy. You nailed it. Thanks for dropping Wilson off, Em. Love that the hair is still understated, Laci."

"Maggie, you're home!" squeals Laci.

"Yup, the prodigal daughter returns. Where's the brief, Jen?"

Jen hands Maggie a one-pager. She and Maggie spend a few minutes reviewing key talking points as Emily and Laci try to peer out the kitchen sink window to see if Sean is in tow. "I think we should walk over and get Cassie, don't you, Laci?" Emily feigns.

"He's out in the driveway talking to Mike. Have at him, girls. I'll text Cassie. I take it she's working from home."

After Emily and Laci head out, Maggie approaches her friend. "Hey, I'm sorry I've been a total shit show the last few days. I was handling everything so well with the divorce and my plans to list the house, he just threw me for a loop, and I didn't handle it well."

"You've needed to be thrown off your flawlessly handling of everything for a long time. I loved it. You were actually vulnerable."

"I guess so, but you wanted to talk about the baby thing, and I didn't listen. I am sorry. Want to grab lunch Friday and talk it out?"

Jen smiles and says, "I'd love to. We've made a decision… We're leaving it up to fate for a year, and then we'll see. So lunch on a regular basis might be in order."

Maggie laughs and says, "Me dating and you contemplating motherhood, we'll have to get a standing reservation at the Grille."

Mike opens the slider and says, "*Fox News* van is pulling up, ladies. You ready?"

They say in unison, "All set!"

Mike turns to go but sticks his head back in and says, "Mags, thumbs-up, girl. Jen, I think we're going to Rehoboth for New Year's."

Maggie smiles back. "I hope *I* get an invite."

Maggie and Jen stroll out into the crisp autumn afternoon in time to catch Cassie heading up her driveway and as another car pulls up. Jen says, "Dex is here with the little ones. She's gonna kill him."

"I got this," Maggie replies, heads over to Mike, and Sean and says, "You two keep the children busy, and that includes Dex, just until we finish taping." She sees their youngest and rethinks it, strolls over to Dex holding his youngest child, and says, "Hey, Sophia, why don't we go see how you come across on camera? You want to come with Ms. Maggie and get some lipstick on?"

The child reaches for her, and Maggie strolls back toward her pals, looking over her shoulder and saying to the men, "Sorry, guys, this is a girl thing."

Maggie heads straight for Bill Anderson. "Hey, Bill, Maggie Burke, nice to see you again. You did a piece on one of my students last year. This is Sophia. We may include her, if you don't mind."

"Right, Maggie, I should have put that together. Good to see you. And we'd love to have Sophia in the shot. We can break if she gets bored." Maggie and Bill wave Jen over, talk lighting and backdrop, and the Reagan patio is selected as their impromptu set. Bill continues, "Give me about five minutes to set this up with my crew. Maggie, I can mic you and one more."

Maggie offers, "Jen, it should be you. You were the brains in all of this."

Jen says, "I'm not comfortable. Just give me a nod in your remarks. I think this may be Laci's moment."

Maggie counters, "Only if I coach her. The moment for crazy has passed. Bill does not have time for that. Am I right, Bill?"

Bill cocks his head asking, "How crazy?"

"We'd better not. I will talk to her. Now, I promised Ms. Sophia some lipstick. Let's go, sweetie." Maggie puts the toddler down and lets her run toward her mother. As she follows, she catches a clear view of Sean talking with four-year-old Matt Holbrecht. Sean holds his hand out as the little boy hands over one of his prized matchbox trucks. Jen is right behind her. "Boys will be boys after all."

As Maggie runs through talking points with Laci, she reminds her to wait for Bill to ask her a question before chiming in. She explains that there are two points to make during the interview and wants to make sure they are not lost amid the somewhat sensational aspects of the story. Cassie asks what the second point is but goes unanswered as Bill is waving them all over.

He positions Emily, Jen, and Cassie in chairs with Laci and Maggie sitting on a half wall directly behind them. Sophia is plopped between them. A little fall foliage remains in Jen's yard assuring the shot will be gorgeous. He encourages Laci and Maggie to speak naturally to him and positions the others to tilt their chairs toward their friends just a bit. "Don't worry about the iPhone taping the conversation. Ready?" The women have their mics, and Laci gives Maggie's hand a squeeze as Bill says, "Rolling."

Laci does a fantastic job explaining how honored she was that the management, staff, and artists at the Purple Parrot allowed her to perform that night. She talks about her desire to authentically represent a group of people prohibited from legalizing their relationships. "It was a big deal to all of us, Bill. We wanted to bring awareness, but we wanted to have a blast doing it because that's who we are. And we had friends like Danny to help us."

Bill turns to Maggie and asks, "But how did you manage to convince an owner of a bar to go along with this over the course of what…a four-day girls' trip?"

Maggie is ready. "Well, first of all, Rehoboth is a great community, very welcoming with a true small-town vibe in the off-season. We met some locals our first day there, which is customary for us. They helped."

She waits for him and then continues, "Look, there were two things in play here. One, a portion of the country has their heads in the sand about same-sex marriage. They need to be told by the Supreme Court that their stance is immoral and illegal moving forward. Who better to approach to ask for help to deliver that message than a man who owns a bar with a weekly drag show?"

Bill takes her bait. "And the second?"

"We are five women who love and respect each other. We each bring unique personalities and talents to all that we do together. Jen was the mastermind and photographer, Cassie kept us on track and got people to dance, Laci has mega talent, and Emily provided encouragement and made sure we had a video to post. When women lift each other up instead of criticizing each other, big things happen."

Bill smiles at her and says, "What did you add, Maggie?"

"I just type fast and have kids in my twenties, so it kind of took off. Oh, and I can be very persuasive."

Bill smiles, turns to the camera, and says, "I'm Bill Anderson. Please retweet these women and #marriageequality, #supremecourt. This has been another story in our series, "'For Goodness' Sake.'

"I have to go, ladies. I want to get this on for the six-o'clock news." And with that, *Fox News* packs up, leaving the men to come up to patio to congratulate their women. Emily calls JT and puts him on speaker. "Girls, tell him, he's at O'Hare, we're going to be on the news!"

Jen grabs the phone ready to read JT the riot act but ends up laughing. JT already set the DVR before he left for the airport this morning. Little Matt Holbrecht walks over to his mother with her silver hair and a baby on her hip and says, "Mom, Ms. Maggie's friend taught me a new word."

The women's heads all swivel instinctively in Matt's direction as Laci calmly asks, "What's that, Matt?"

The little boy smiles directly at Sean and proudly says, "Harley."

Maggie shakes her head as Sean and Matt high five and whispers in Laci's ear, "I told you he was a bad boy."

CHAPTER 24

Laci

Maggie called Laci a week after the broadcast to ask her for coffee. Laci fears she is closing herself off from seeing Sean and has asked the other women to join her after a half hour or so. If Maggie is really going to screw this up, she will have to explain it to all of them. Ultimately, it is Maggie's decision, but a little peer pressure might help.

She spots Maggie as soon as she enters Starbucks, laptop up and typing furiously away. Laci walks to her table, leans over, and slowly closes the screen. "Not on my time, Maggie."

She pushes it back. "Just two minutes. I'm midemail, and you're late. Go order."

The laptop is closed when Laci returns. "Where's your drink?"

"They're bringing it to me."

Maggie gives her a puzzled look until a young man with a flawless manicure delivers Laci's grande blonde roast and two slices of pumpkin loaf. "Pumpkin loaf on the house, ladies. Any friend of Laci's is a friend of mine!"

Laci beams in his direction. "Thanks, Jason, but this has to stop. You're going to get in trouble." After he is back behind the counter, she turns to Maggie and asks, "Is this happening to you? I am getting free stuff wherever I go. It's nuts, and unfortunately the kids are starting to expect it."

Maggie chuckles and says, "No, and I'm happy flying under the radar. Besides, you are the face of our campaign. Enjoy the fame while you have it. It will all blow over in a week or so."

They exchange plans for Thanksgiving Day, which provides the opportunity for Laci to ask, "Long weekend. Any plans with Sean?"

"Heading down on Friday. I think Patrick is driving down with me. He is determined to lay eyes on him, which I find very hypocritical of him. He has a fit every time I ask to meet his latest. I suppose if I met every guy he mentions he's seeing, I'd have to move to Boston."

Laci is relieved to hear about the plans. She knows the weekend after their trip was tied up with a wedding of one of Maggie's nieces. "Patrick's just protective, Maggie. And probably carrying out his sisters' orders."

"Definitely. Anyway I need to talk to you about something. Promise me you'll hear me out before you kick into full-throttle problem-solving mode."

"Okay, but I have to answer a text real quick, and then I will shut my phone down." Laci shoots a quick group text out.

"**ABORT INTERVENTION...all good.**"

As Laci puts her phone away, Maggie launches into the truth about Danny. She gives her a detailed account of her visit to the shelter, his dodgy behavior, and the explanation from Sr. Jeanne that he has lived there for six years. "Honestly, Laci, I have no idea how child services didn't get involved. I mean, raised by nuns... That is going to take years of therapy. I'm guessing he went to Catholic school, wherever that is down there."

Laci has tears in her eyes. "His mother just left him?"

"Again, I'm guessing here because ole Jeanne was pretty tight-lipped, but I'd say drugs."

Maggie then launches into her plan to get Danny further educated. She stresses the importance of holding him accountable because people find him either charming or feel sorry for him. "Personally, I've wanted to wring his neck on more than one occasion. He needs to do this himself, Laci, which does not mean he does not need mothering. So I'm asking if you can be a part of this... He needs encouragement mixed with culpability."

"Oh, I am so going to ride his ass."

"Good, one more thing…and I'm on the fence about telling you this part."

"If you want me to help, you have to tell me."

Maggie takes a deep breath. "He was hooking on the Boardwalk."

Laci reaches into bag and pulls out her phone. Maggie grabs her arm. "Hold up. He promised he would stop. I am just not sure who can keep an eye on him. Clearly Sean is clueless. He is as bad as the nuns are. Giving him odd jobs, letting him stay at the shelter and not be on time for work. I will be addressing all of that. But who can be our eyes down there?"

Laci is thinking. "You know, Farrah did my hair that night, and he's a great guy. I can text him and see if we can set up a call to discuss some options for schools. As for keeping an eye on him… I think Jesse has potential. They are actually friends. I think Danny was in his little sister's class."

"I can always count on you for two things, getting a drag queen's digits and finding connections. Well, this is a good start. You set up the call. I'll see Danny this weekend and see where he is with his applications."

"Okay, but can I go ahead and text him that I know everything?"

"Your call. I am also worried about heroin, but his arms looked clean. Doesn't mean he doesn't snort it or worse. I'd also like your thoughts on bringing the other girls into the loop."

"Let them be the encouragement, Maggie. They don't need to know this stuff. He's going to need all kinds of love, not just tough love."

They come up with a plan for the five of them to pull together a Christmas package filled with things he will need for school. Laci and Dex will make sure he receives it before the twenty-fifth. "We can put the kids in the van, and they'll be knocked out until we get there. It might be the first private conversation we'll have all month!"

Maggie smiles thinking of her empty nest and reminds her friend that she will miss these days when they are gone. Talk turns to Maggie listing her house in the New Year. She hopes Laci believes she was ready to sell long before she met Sean. "It's too hard to move on when you are living with the memories. Sweet as most of them were, the tough ones can erode them."

"I'm proud of you, Maggie. Too many couples hate each other when it's over. You and Kevin somehow kept a friendship."

"Of course we did. We have three great kids and had a pretty good life together. Look, I love the guy, but we both let the romance die. He needs to try and find that with someone else, and apparently, so do I."

"I'm pretty sure you have."

"Guess what, me too. Yikes!"

Coffee cups are recycled and heartfelt hugs exchanged before the women head out to the pre-Thanksgiving hustle.

CHAPTER 25

Cassie

Cassie trolls the aisles at Wegman's at seven thirty on a Thursday evening in search of something that is non-holiday specific, non-food allergy, non-trans fat for Jon's nonholiday party tomorrow at school. She lands on organic tortilla chips with jars of green and red salsa. She turns to head toward check out and hears a voice coming around the corner. "Cassie, is that you? I haven't seen you since Rehoboth."

All she can think is *Shit! This going to add ten minutes onto my quick trip to the store.*

"Hi, Heather, just getting stuff for Jon's party tomorrow before I have to pick him up from basketball practice. I don't mean to be rude, but I don't want to be late for pickup."

Heather now has her cart alongside Cassie's and angled in a way so Cassie can't get around without knocking it over. "Oh, I won't keep you. I have to say you girls really looked like you had a great time down there. I heard Jen was body surfing in a sea of gay men."

"Yeah, pretty much. It was the only way she could get to the dance floor."

"And Laci...well, is anyone really surprised?" Cassie is starting to jiggle her cart as Heather continues, "But what I really want to know, is Maggie still seeing that biker dude? Does he even hold a steady job?"

"Actually, Heather, I wouldn't worry about his job, he's pretty successful. Owns a restaurant, is very community minded, has a beautiful home there. As far as them being together, let's just say the cows have not come home yet."

Heather gets herself in a huff and starts to respond, "Well, she just looks like a tramp. Everyone thinks—" Another shopper comes down the aisle in front of them, pushing her mini cart loaded with red wine and dogfish lager. Her glare would melt an iceberg.

"Hi, Cassie. It would appear some people have short memories and even less self-awareness. And I warned you about this." There are now two more women in the aisle, and Maggie loves an audience, so she continues, "Heather, you nosy, petty bitch, you really need to go fuck yourself." She reaches over to Cassie's cart and rattles it until Heather's cart starts to topple over. Heather grabs it, but not before her toilet paper and chips fall out of her cart, to which Maggie dryly replies, "Oops. There you go, Cassie, now you are no longer entrapped by a woman with nothing nice to say about anyone." The two other women in the aisle are smiling to themselves as Maggie wheels past them.

They catch up in the parking lot. "Oh my god, why did I not tape that? The others are going to be so jealous."

"That's okay, Cassie, the telling of it is half the fun."

"I think I know who you are shopping for. When's he coming up?"

"Tonight. Patrick comes in for break tomorrow. I have a few donor calls to make in the morning, spend some time with Patrick, and then we will hit the road so Sean can be back for the dinner crowd. You should see how Becca has the place decorated for the holidays."

"Well, I will. I'm coming for New Year's Eve."

"Awesome! A plus one?"

"I'm working on it. I have a dinner date tomorrow night."

"Atta girl. Have fun, and listen, don't be late for your son."

Cassie gets in her van with appreciation for her friend that did not drill her for a million details. Then she laughs to herself and thinks she would have been surprised if she had.

*****

Cassie hears bickering downstairs and hopes the house will be standing when she gets back. She would intervene with a stern warning, but she is not leaving for another fifteen minutes. Why waste her breath? She finishes her makeup as Emma comes into her bathroom holding a slip of paper. "Mom, why are you putting makeup on to go Christmas shopping with Dad?"

"Because there are too many mirrors in King of Prussia Mall and I don't want to scare myself. Whatcha got there, Emma?"

"I thought I would organize my list by convenience at the mall, like, you are probably parking outside Nordstrom's, upper level, right?"

"Okay, sure."

"Well, as you walk out of Nordstrom's, you're right at Abercrombie and Fitch, where the bomber jacket I want is. It's in the back and chained to the rack."

"Emma, you know if you get that it's the only present you are getting for Christmas, which is kind of stupid because they will be half off on the twenty-sixth and 70 percent off January first."

"Oh, Mom, they'll be gone by then. Anyway, here's the rest of my list. Dad says he really wants to get me the jacket. So you can focus on the rest."

"You understand that your parents get along, right? We do this together for a reason...because we'd like to be able to send you to college someday."

Before Emma can offer a rebuttal, they hear a thunderous. "Mom! Dad's here!"

"Mom, did you drop him on his head when he was a baby? I swear, he's a moron."

She stuffs Emma's list in her purse and asks her to be civil to her brother for the couple of hours she'll be gone. When she gets to the kitchen, she sees that Doug has also been handed a list. Judging by the fact that it is written on a paper towel, she assumes it belongs to Jon. She gives Jon a hug, asking him to be decent to his sister. His response, "Bring me home dessert?"

As they drive the twenty minutes to King of Prussia, they review what has been ordered and shipped to her parents' house for safekeeping. The best part of having retired parents is most of the gifts will be wrapped when Doug picks them up on the twenty-third. He asks, "We doing Christmas Eve at your parents this year?"

They finish the rest of the ride mapping out Christmas Day and the day after. Ever since their divorce, Doug has spent Christmas Eve and all of Christmas Day with Cassie and the kids. Cassie cannot imagine it would ever be any different. The mall is packed. Cassie gives Doug Emma's parking suggestion, and sure enough, they find a spot. She wonders if she should worry about her daughter's intimate knowledge of the King of Prussia Mall.

After an hour and a half of shopping, they settle in at their table at the Cheesecake Factory, and a server approaches them for their cocktail order. "We have margarita specials tonight."

Cassie replies, "No thanks. A Corona Light please. I saw what tequila can do to a woman firsthand, and it's not pretty." Doug smiles and asks for a Yuengling.

After the beers are delivered, he asks how this all happened in Rehoboth. Cassie tries to do the story justice without giving too many details. They are on their second beer when dinner arrives and the story has covered up to the volleyball game. After the server leaves, she does a fast forward to the Parrot, making Laci the center of the story. "And then we packed up and came home. But Maggie is still seeing him."

"I'm pretty sure I'm not getting everything. I'll have to compare notes with Mike."

"I guarantee he's gotten less out of Jen. Look, Doug, no one saw this coming, especially Maggie. But that guy was all about her from the moment he saw her. I just don't think he knew what he was getting himself into. The thing is, they are great together."

"Did they hook up?"

"What do you think? Of course they did."

He leans in across the table to ask, "Have you ever done that on one of these trips?"

Suddenly she feels flattered. "Well, no. No one has. I am telling you, it was like nothing I have ever seen before…like a twenty-car pileup where everyone walks out unharmed. And everyone who witnessed the wreck is like, 'That was amazing.'"

"So you think this is real?"

"One hundred percent. She is not hiding anything, still bossy, quick-tempered, and honest-to-a-fault Maggie. He is aloof, hard to gauge, but there is some kind of balance there. In addition, there is the chemistry…huge chemistry. He is a great guy, and you will get it if you ever see them together. You know, she said something to me when we were down there. I asked her if it was awkward, and she said if you feel like it's awkward, it's not the right time or right guy."

Doug smiles at her and says, "Makes sense to me. It was never awkward for us."

Cassie feels herself blushing and says, "It was once when my mother walked in on us." They both howl at the memory.

They finish dinner, order two desserts to go, and walk through the mall to where he parked his car. He gets her door, which does not go unnoticed. As they head back to Chester Springs, he says, "This was a really nice night." She agrees, and then he completely surprises her and asks, "Would you do it again, minus the shopping?"

Before she can think about it, she says, "Yeah, I'd like that."

"How about next Saturday night?"

"It's a date."

CHAPTER 26

Sean, December 2014

Sean DeMarco drives to Chester County on December 30, anxious to beat an imminent snowstorm and pick up Maggie for a long weekend in Rehoboth. He has decided he should purchase a third vehicle because these trips are not stopping anytime soon.

The drive to her has become something he looks forward to, peace mixed with anticipation followed by the warmth he finds in her company. He has learned she absolutely cannot carry a tune, loves to dance in the car, laugh at people on the road, and quietly confide in him about her worries at work, the sale of her house, or the world at large. She is every bit as smart as he first thought and extremely intuitive. Her sense of timing is impeccable, which is why he went along with her plans for today.

Today he meets her daughters. He remembers meeting Pat on Black Friday. Pat and Maggie hit the outlets and then met him for dinner. A member of Pat's team from Tufts has a family house down in Fenwick and was hosting a party Saturday night. They connected quickly over music and difficult professors, and Pat ended up agreeing to stay over at Sean's before heading to Fenwick the next day. Since then there have been conversations over speakerphone in the car or at halftime of the Eagles games, all very easy.

The girls, however, leave him feeling perplexed. True to style, she has said little about them, protecting their privacy and leaving the impressions solely up to Sean.

He turns the Jeep onto Maggie's long, winding road, and as it curves to the right, he passes two twenty-somethings running together, one taller, both with ponytails swinging as they run, headbands covering their ears and oblivious to him. He passes them and sees them look directly at each other, and he knows the Burke girls have spotted him.

As he approaches her house, he smiles at the fact that Maggie's driveway looks like a used-car parking lot. He parks the Jeep on the street and leans in to move things around in the back seat. He hears the quickened pace of the girls in sprint mode and closes up the Jeep. One of them outruns her sister, stops at their mailbox, bends over, and coughs in the cold. The other is five feet away from him and casually says "Hey" before ripping the top off her water bottle and draining the contents.

He sees Maggie in this girl, which means this is Lindsey. No sooner than that thought is completed then he hears, "Hi, I'm Caroline. That slowpoke there is my sister, Lindsey."

Lindsey wipes her forehead and says, "Cool car." Caroline shoots her a disapproving look.

"Hi, girls, I'm Sean."

Lindsey responds, "Yeah, great to meet you. No need to make this weird. Mom's got breakfast going. See ya inside." She heads across their lawn to the front door.

Caroline calls after her, "Lindsey, you suck. And I beat you, Ms. All-American."

"Yeah, I know. I let you. Couldn't take the whining." She turns to look at her sister, then Lindsey flashes a smile at Sean, and he thinks Jen was right. She is Maggie's mini-me.

Caroline begins, "Hope you're hungry. She makes the best breakfast. Excuse us, it's a full house in there. A few people stayed over last night." Instead of crossing over the lawn, she walks in the direction of the driveway, so he follows.

She stops three-quarters of the way down the driveway, which leaves him highly amused because there is no direct site line from any windows or doors of the house. She begins, "Listen, before we go inside, I need to say a couple of things."

He sees the Maggie command for respect in this girl and happily complies. "What's on your mind?"

"Linds and I had coffee with the girls yesterday, so we kind of get it. At least get it more than what my mother's bullet points reveal. That said, I know she cares about you, and that is enough for us. But do us a favor and don't take that lightly."

Caroline continues, "She's been alone a long time. My dad is a good guy, but she…well, she's our mother. He did his thing, and she did hers, which was to raise us in a way that we never noticed how much she did by herself. So don't ever let her feel lonely, because she deserves more than that."

"It won't be a problem."

"One more thing… Pat, Linds, and I, we come first with her. That is not our choice. It is hers. If you can't handle that, you'll have to figure it out."

Now Sean looks her dead in the eyes. She flinches just a bit at the intensity of his gaze and stance as he says, "Caroline, you three should come first. We do not have our parents long enough no matter how old they are when they leave us. So cherish her because you're luckier than you know."

Caroline tilts her head, eyes wide, and smiles at him to say, "Good talk, Sean. Let's go eat. I'm famished." As if on cue, Maggie opens the front door. Wilson bounds out running toward Caroline, circles Sean, and drops a ball at his feet.

Caroline walks in as her mother walks out to greet Sean. "So those are my girls. I'm thinking Lindsey was indifferent and Caroline was protective. I just hope neither was rude."

"Not at all. And I'd give you a kiss, but there are eyes upon us from your living room." He tosses the ball to Wilson, and the three of them head inside.

The crowd inside consists of Maggie's children and their current romantic interests. A gorgeous breakfast of eggs, grilled ham, home fries, and crumb cake is on the table along with coffee, fresh orange juice, and ice water. Her farmhouse table is fully extended in order to fit the crowd.

As five men file into the kitchen, Caroline says to her mother, "This is not good. We are officially outnumbered."

Maggie responds, smiling, and says, "Well, somebody has to stop bringing men home."

Patrick pipes in first, "You know that's not going to be me, right?" Lindsey smacks him on the back of his head and gives his boyfriend, Joey, a hug before sitting down next to Will. It is another boisterous breakfast in Maggie's kitchen filled with talk about plans for New Year's Eve.

Sean and Patrick tackle the cleanup while Maggie drills her daughters on their plans. Lindsey reports she is heading to NYC with Will for the third consecutive year to revel in the mayhem that is New Year's Eve in the city. After the usual requests for a text when they get home to their college friends' apartment, the two of them head upstairs to pack up and hit the road. Caroline is noncommittal as Jack tosses a dozen ideas around. Maggie thinks this boy is on borrowed time.

Patrick and Joey are dog sitting, a.k.a., having people over, and Maggie is certain Caroline will be hanging with her brother more than she will be with Jack. Maggie goes up to finish packing her bag, and Caroline follows her. "Hey Mom, need help?"

"Nope, but I always like the company. Come on up." Once back in her room, Caroline unravels as Maggie throws scarves and accessories into her bag.

"Mom, I think I'm gonna break up with Jack."

"Tonight? That's kind of harsh, isn't it?"

"Well, like right after you leave, actually."

"Oh my god, Caroline, cut the poor kid a break. It's the holidays. Just fake it till the second week of January and then call it a day. He just bought you that beautiful bag for Christmas."

"All right…" She quickly changes the subject. "Are all the girls going tomorrow night?"

"Yup." Maggie explains who is staying where and admits, "At least the husbands will be with them, so it should be a little tamer."

"Umm, Mom…they aren't the ones that came back with a boyfriend." With that, Maggie throws a pair of socks at her daughter, and they enjoy a good laugh over the dynamics at the breakfast table.

*****

Sean and Maggie hit Rehoboth by five. Snow had started to fall while they were heading south on 95, and the Coastal Highway has a more than a coating. "You have to be tired. Up and back in a day, what a drag. Who would ask you to do such a thing?"

He teases, "The woman who is buying the pizza, that's who."

"You're on! Fire made by any chance?"

"Yup, and a bottle of wine already out. Let it snow. I got my woman and my dog. I don't need to go anywhere."

Once settled back at Sean's, shoes off and fire lit, they call Jim to ask him to come over for pizza. Maggie watches him from the front windows and meets him on the front porch to make sure he does not slip on the thin layer of snow. "You don't have shoes on, Maggie. Get inside!"

Sean answers, "It's a thing with her, Jim. She never knows where her shoes are."

Pizza and a bottle of Barolo later, the trio get down to figuring where everyone will sleep. Jim's house has four bedrooms, Sean's, three, but one is an office. Maggie suggests Jim stay with them, but he declines as he has been looking forward to hosting the couples for weeks. After enough last-minute trades to rival the NFL Draft, the couples all have assigned houses and rooms.

As Jim puts on his coat and Sean bundles up to walk him back, Maggie brings a tin of chocolate chip cookies over to Jim and says, "Merry Christmas, Jim. Don't eat them all at once."

When Sean returns, Maggie sees a touch of sorrow in his eyes and asks, "You thinking about tomorrow? It's thirty years, isn't it?"

"Maybe a little, but I'm worried about Jim too. I feel like this was our last Christmas together. He's slowing down, and I know he's entitled to, but he's been my best friend. It's hard to accept he's aging."

"You can't predict any of that, Sean. You would break his heart if he sensed your concern. He loves you too much to let you worry about him." She pauses. "And I do too."

He wraps her in a hug. "I've been waiting for that, you know. Not a simple 'I love you,' but I have learned to be patient."

"Can't give it to you all at once, DeMarco. I really don't think you could handle it."

*****

The next morning Sean fights the day ahead, eyes closed, not willing himself to get up yet. He always struggles to remember Edwin privately before heading into work to create the celebration of life that Tony started the year after Edwin passed. Tony was so sick himself by that time, yet Darby's was alive with music and friends coming together to create a fantastic party. Sean wonders if it means the same to anyone anymore.

He hears her bare footsteps climbing the stairs and smells coffee as she quietly enters the room. She places it on the cedar coaster, where his water glass was, and smiles at him as he opens his eyes. Maggie understands the conflict in this man today, a business to take care of amid the memory of a very personal loss. His world had begun to crumble this day thirty years ago. She suspects it was Edwin, who had the foresight to secure Sean's future financially. He knew Sean would lose his brother to the same horrific disease all too soon, within a mere eighteen months.

She sits on the edge of the bed. "Time to get up. It's after eight thirty."

"Whoa… I never sleep this late." He sits up. "Rosie must need to go out."

"Already taken care of." Maggie hands him his coffee before she begins, "This is going be a late night. It's a good thing you slept in. Besides, I suspect today is not your favorite day of the year. Soooo I think we should hit the beach for a bit."

"It didn't snow?"

"No, it did, and we need to get down there before it all melts. It's going to be magical."

"You've lost your mind."

"It's debatable I ever had one... Now get moving. I have something nice planned for you."

Fifteen minutes later, he is in the kitchen looking for a second cup of coffee, and he sees her bundled in down coat, knit hat, and gloves with a brown bag in her hand. His jacket, hat, and gloves are on the couch. "Do I hear the Jeep out?"

"Yup, I'm driving."

They head out, and she opens the door for him on the passenger side, which he finds typically ridiculous of her. Rather than ask where they are going, he happily lets her run the show. Within minutes, he has figured out. They are going to Henelopen Park. He takes in the snowcapped roofs and Christmas decor and thinks she is right. It is a beautiful site. She continues through the park to the site of the Cape May Lewes Ferry and parks in the empty lot.

She reaches for the brown bag in the back of the Jeep and pulls out her props. There is a glass bottle with about three inches of gold glitter in the bottom, two pieces of parchment, and two pens. "I'd like to write a note to Edwin. I never got to meet him, and I want to thank him because I see his influence on you in your relationship with Jesse. Might be nice if you add one too."

He leans over to give her a kiss, takes the paper and pen, and says, "If you drop that glitter in this car, you're in big trouble."

"What's with the glitter hatred? I am paying homage to his designs for *Dream Girls*. I wish Laci were here. She would have gotten that."

"No offense, I'm glad she's not."

When he finishes writing, he asks her for her note, places them together without reading hers, and rolls them into a tight scroll. Maggie uncorks the bottle and carefully places them inside. She stops for a minute, looks him straight in the eye, and says, "I *really* want to shake this all over your car, but I won't."

"Thank you."

She pops in the cork, opens her door, tosses him the keys, and makes her way to the jetty. He has no choice but to follow her in the snow. She waits on the beach for him to catch up, taking in the glistening snow by the dunes as she looks down beach. Her mind wanders to a twenty-seven-year-old man faced with the impending loss of his only brother with no cure in sight for the disease that was probably ravaging Tony's body as much as Edwin's death had broken his heart.

When he arrives, she explains, "We're going out as far as we can, and then you're going to hold on to me so I don't slip when I toss this into the ocean."

"Maybe I should toss it."

"Nope, I want you thinking about Edwin and ask him to let you know he's around today, got it?"

"I'm game, but we stop when I think we're far enough, okay?"

She nods in agreement. They make it about two-thirds of the way out on the jetty. He sees the rocks taking on more water and stops her. Rather than fight him, she keeps her agreement. She puts her arms around him and asks if he is ready. "Turn around," he says. "Now give me a minute, and stop fidgeting." After a moment, his arms tighten around her a bit, and he says, "Okay, on three…one, two, three."

Maggie sends the bottle in a slightly arched spiral pass. They watch it twirl over the ocean, and as it hits the water, a spray of glitter shoots out of the top. She turns to him laughing and says, "Well, that was fast. I thought you'd get your sign at Darby's tonight." She secretly tucks the cork in her pocket and takes his hand as they make their way to the Jeep.

By two o'clock, the troops are pulling in. The couples are greeted with welcome bags containing cookies, water, room assignments, and an itinerary. Each woman receives a five-by-seven wrapped frame, which they promptly open together. Emily has torn through hers first and walks over to give Maggie a hug as the others delight in the photograph of them holding hands as they slid past the last crest of the three-story slide. True enough, Laci did get air.

194

The women share holiday stories over wine and hors d'oeuvres, and a game plan for the night comes together. Emily and JT are staying at Sean's. The others are equally happy to spend time with Jim. Emily, however, does not miss the opportunity to boast, "That's because I'm Sean's favorite."

"No kidding," confirms Maggie. "I think you were on to us early. And you had a major impact on not letting me self-sabotage."

Cassie delivers her usual quip, "Seriously, Mags? That took *all* of us."

By four, all scatter to relax, except Maggie and Sean. Sean promoted Becca to general manager and Jesse to food and beverage manager before Christmas. Although he is trying to stay out of their way, he wants to get there in time to be an extra set of hands. Maggie has promised Becca she would stall him until five and then help as needed.

An hour later, Sean is pacing downstairs dressed in his Seven jeans and J.Hilburn custom shirt, anxiously waiting for Maggie. He hears JT give a wolf whistle and Emily say, "You are such a clothes horse! And those shoes!"

He sees the black suede high heels and black velvet jeans first, but the champagne organza wrap blouse over the gold silk camisole stops him cold. Her hair is in a soft Hollywood wave, tucked on one side with a gold glittered pin, her lips are red, and her eyes have a dusting of light charcoal. She twirls around for him as she walks toward him as he simply says, "Wow."

He refuses to take her through the kitchen at Darby's. As they enter the bar, a new bartender is taking care of some of the early regulars. He helps her off with her coat, putting it over his arm. Every man swivels, and she stops to say hello to most of them as he keeps moving. One of his best customers, Bob, yells after him, "Seriously, dude, you're just gonna leave her here by me? She may not be here when you get back."

"Not really worried about it, Bob!"

She smiles and thinks, *Still so cocky.* She is enjoying the conversation with his most loyal clientele when something catches her eye by the register. A moment later Jesse is under the service bar and asking her for a drink order. "Club soda, Jess. It's too early for me to start."

She leaves her drink next to Bob and asks him to watch it for a moment. She sees some early birds in for dinner and smiles at them. Becca comes out from the kitchen. "Great outfit, and you look awesome! I didn't see Sean…" Maggie points to the office.

"Need any help in the other room?"

"Oh my god, yes. Let me check in with him, and I'll be over in ten minutes or so."

Maggie thinks the poor kid is understandably frazzled. It is a big night for Becca. Maggie heads back to her drink at the bar and is entertained by two of the guys when she sees it again at the register. She does not change her expression or neglect the men she is talking to, but her mind is racing. Jesse is in the dining room, just having seated a couple. She tries to get his attention, but he is doing exactly what he should, making the guests feel welcome on a very busy night.

The new bartender comes over to their group looking to freshen drinks. He looks directly at Maggie and says, "You're new here."

Bob laughs and says, "No, Einstein, you are. That's your boss's gal." Maggie offers nothing, and neither does the bartender. That is all the proof she needs.

Sean and Becca exit the office and head to the larger dining room. Maggie excuses herself to go help with decorations. Sean immediately notices her, his pace slowing down get a better look at her. She seems upset in some way. As they approach her, she quietly says, "I need to talk to you two. Let's go over by the stage."

"Great, that's where the boxes are anyway," Becca naively responds. Maggie now has Sean's full attention.

Maggie smiles warmly at them. "Becca, honey, forget about the boxes for a minute. You guys have a little problem." As they approach the stage, she asks if the mics are live. Sean reaches up, touches one, dead.

He asks, "Now what's up?"

"Your new bartender is stealing from you. I saw it twice. Beers are five bucks, right?"

Becca answers, "Domestic, yeah."

"Well, he's taking the customer's ten or twenty and giving them their change, but not ringing it as a sale. Instead, he puts a tally on a piece of paper next to the register and grabs a five for his tip jar. It's New Year's Eve. No one is going to pay attention to him."

Becca is in shock. Sean adds, "Except someone did. Becca, go get Jesse…now." His eyes are as dark as she has ever seen them, and she has made them very dark at times. He asks Maggie to repeat what she said and then asks Jesse to go behind the bar to get them both a club soda. "Get a glimpse at the tip jar." He nods at the women, adding, "You two, start unpacking those boxes please."

Becca offers, "I can handle this, Sean. I'm your GM."

"It's still my money, Becca. When it's yours, you may have the pleasure."

Maggie starts laying out party hats and noisemakers alongside a dejected Becca. She gives her a reassuring look and looks back at Sean. He is seething. She needs to get him out of sight and weakly offers, "Sean, I think a string is broken on your guitar."

He turns toward her as if she has lost her mind and sees the "get over here" look in her eyes. As he approaches, she says, "Stop staring at him or he's going to put all the money back. What you have to decide is if you need him to get through tonight regardless of the couple hundred it may cost you."

Jesse returns with the drinks. "I've worked that bar for three years and never had a tip jar like that before ten o'clock. He's skimming."

Sean bluntly asks, "Who hired him?"

Jesse says, "I did, Sean."

"Okay, managers, this is how is goes down here. Whoever hires fires. Becca, your focus right now is to figure out who's running your dining room, who's watching your kitchen, and who's tending bar when Jesse comes up on stage."

"Sean, I've already tweeted music at ten. Is that still on?"

"Yup. I have every confidence in you, Becca. You will figure it out. Jesse, you have exactly two minutes to get that punk out of my place before I pull him over the bar and kick his ass all the way to the curb."

Maggie turns away from Sean, looks at Becca, flutters her hand over her heart, and whispers, "Oh my god, he is so hot right now." Becca puts her head down for fear of laughing.

Becca does figure it out. She asks Maggie to hostess. She will take the kitchen and the small dining room, and Sean will work the crowd with an eye on helping Jesse at the bar when it starts getting packed. When the band goes on stage, the bar will have coverage. She will have an extra barback that comes on at eight.

Maggie offers, "Can we drag Jesse's start time to ten thirty? It would help the kitchen get the entrees out if everyone stays on the floor till then."

Sean smiles at her, intuitive and smart. He also saw her little antic when she turned around earlier, so he adds *sassy* to his mental list.

Maggie fills the role as hostess like she is back in her dad's tavern. The place is quickly filling up with both regulars and a few new friends. Rick and Jay from DC come in, and she notices the newlyweds have no reservation. She greets them at the bar and asks if they would like to sit with her group as she will not be able to join the table until late. Her crew arrives next, shocked to see her grabbing menus and taking people to their seats.

As she returns to seat them, she gets a little surprise. "Doug, you're joining us! It's great to see you." She shoots a look to Jen, who gives her a "don't ask me" look in return. Cassie steps up, "Nothing to see here, Maggie. We took the room with the twin beds."

She teases Doug, "That shouldn't stop you. But please be respectful, Jim is in his eighties, after all, so keep it down."

Her friends have turned it out for the occasion, one prettier than the next. She happily watches the chemistry at their table as she fills the dining room with patrons and starts running drink orders once the tables are at capacity. At ten fifteen, she approaches her friends. "The bar is about to close for twenty minutes or so. How about I bring over a round?" She writes down everyone's orders, and when she comes to Laci, she hears, "Just water, thanks."

Maggie drops her pen, looks at her friend, and says, "Oh my god, you're pregnant."

"Yeah, I never took the pasties off when I went home last year because I wanted to show Dex, and well, here we are."

Jen groans, Emily claps, Maggie winks at Dex, and Cassie says, "Shit, now I have to tell Doug about the pasties."

Maggie sees Sean pacing on the side of the dining room. She smiles at him and points to Laci and tries to mouth "Big news," but he cannot make out what she is trying to say. Maggie runs to the bar, grabs bottles of beer for the men and a bottle of champagne for the women, and asks the new barback, Danny, to help deliver the drink orders she has left behind. When she arrives at the table, she shoves an empty seat between JT and Emily and exhales while Em hands her champagne. Emily asks, "Maggie, are you going back into the restaurant business?"

She laughs and emphatically says, "Not a chance! I mean, these heels are not meant for this kind of work. But Becca was in a jam, and I am sleeping with the owner. Besides, you know I love it when a man owes me."

Jesse and Mac step on stage. When they settle in, Jesse begins strumming and says, "New Year's Eve is full of traditions, we have a one here. Someone used to open with this, but one night he saved it for last, and the woman he wanted to impress the most almost killed him. So tonight we're putting it back where it belongs and opening with it."

"It's rainin' but there ain't a cloud in the sky
Musta been a tear from your eye
Everything'll be okay…

Sean makes his way to Maggie, stands behind her, and leans over to whisper in her ear, "Thank you for stepping in to help tonight. You good?"

"Best I've been in a long time." She senses his nervousness for his protégé and continues, "Now, look at Jesse up there… I think you've been replaced."

"You know what? It's about time." He and Jim are working on a profit-sharing plan for Becca and Jesse to begin after their first year in their new roles. While he will always remain a principle, he has other things he would like to do with his life. Perhaps get a master's degree, travel, and do more things for himself, starting with spending more time with her.

Sean grabs a Dogfish from the bucket of beers as Mike approaches to congratulate him on creating a great New Year's Eve. "There's something special about this place, but I can't quite pinpoint it. Is it the music, the food, the patrons? It's like the whole spirit of the place."

Maggie smiles at Jen and says to Mike, "It might be the Manhattans you are drinking, but sure, we'll go with spirit of the place."

With that, Mike leans into Maggie's ear and says, "Listen here, you, don't screw this up. You are more than just sleeping with the guy. You are fooling no one." He kisses her on the cheek and grabs Jen's hand, and they hit the dance floor. Maggie sees Cassie and Doug are up next, and she and Sean exchange looks. The other couples are right behind them.

Maggie pats the chair next to her, and Sean sits with a sigh of a fifty-five-year-old man who has been running around his restaurant for five straight hours. She faces him and asks, "The question is, are you good?"

When he looks into her eyes, she sees the depth of his losses. She puts her hand in his, remembering how his touch calmed her when her emotions got the best of her that initial weekend in November. Their connection, swift and strong. Sean leans in, kisses her, and says, "Best I've ever been, truly."

He shifts his gaze to her glass, and his demeanor changes as he hands it to her. Maggie sees the source of his amusement: glitter from someone's hat or outfit floats in her champagne. She silently thanks Edwin for the sign. She stands and seductively bends down to whisper in his ear, "How pissed would everyone be if I asked you to sneak me out the back?"

"Way ahead of you, Maggie."

Waitin' on a Sunny Day

Bruce Springsteen

It's rainin', but there ain't a cloud in the sky
Musta been a tear from your eye
Everything'll be okay
Funny, thought I felt a sweet summer breeze
Musta been you sighin' so deep
Don't worry we're gonna find a way

I'm waitin', waitin' on a sunny day
Gonna chase the clouds away
I'm waiting on a sunny day

Without you I'm workin' with the rain fallin' down
I'm half a party in a one-dog town
I need you to chase the blues away
Without you I'm a drummer that can't keep a beat
An ice cream truck on a deserted street
I hope that you're coming to stay

I'm waitin', waitin' on a sunny day
Gonna chase the clouds away
I'm waiting on a sunny day

Hard times, baby, well, they come to us all
Sure as the tickin' of the clock on the wall
Sure as the turning of night into day
But your smile, girl, brings the mornin' light to my eyes
Lifts away the blues when I rise
I hope that you are comin' to stay

I'm waitin', waitin' on a sunny day
Gonna chase the clouds away
I'm waiting on a sunny day

This story was inspired by some of the people and places I know and the lyrics in this song. It is all a work of fiction with no direct correlation to true events, mostly.

Maggie's Buzzed Butternut Squash Apple Soup

Prep Time	15 minutes
Cook Time	45 minutes
Total Time	60 minutes
Servings	6 servings

Ingredients

For the soup:
I medium yellow onion, chopped (1 cup +/-)
1 celery rib, chopped (3/4 cup)
1 carrot, copped (3/4 cup)
2 TB unsalted butter
1 butternut squash, peeled, seeded and chopped (6 to 8 cups)
1 large tart green apple, peeled, cored, chopped (2 cups)
3 cups chicken stock or broth (substitution: vegetable broth)
1 cup water
1/3 cup Crown Royal Vanilla Bourbon
Pinches of: nutmeg, cinnamon, cayenne, salt and pepper

Suggestions for the garnish:
(all Optional)
Fresh parsley, chopped
Chives, chopped
Dash of smoked paprika
Sour Cream
Chopped Walnuts
Thinly sliced skin on green apple wedges to float on top arranged as flower petals

Method

1. Sauté onion, carrot celery in butter:

   Heat a large thick-bottomed pot on medium-high heat.
   Melt butter in the pot and let it foam up and recede.
   Add the onion, carrot and celery and sauté for 5 minutes.
   Lower the heat if the heat if the vegetables begin to brown

2. Cook the soup:

   Add the butternut squash, apple, broth, and water. Bring to a boil.
   Reduce to a simmer, cover, and simmer for 30 minutes or so until squash and carrots have softened.

3. Purée the soup:

   Use an immersion blender to purée the soup, or work in batches to purée in a standard blender.
   Add seasonings and bourbon, salt and pepper to taste.
   Pour into warmed bowls and garnish as preferred.

Maria McKeon is a lifelong resident of Chester County, Pennsylvania. She was raised in a large traditional Irish American household and is the daughter of a successful restauranteur who became one of the premiere caterers in the greater Philadelphia area, where she began her career as a high-end event planner. Growing up in her family's dining establishments fostered her love of food, wine, and decor.

At the age of thirty-two, she left the family business to forge her own career, centered in the nonprofit sector. Her experience spans thirty years, working for a variety of organizations as large as the University of Pennsylvania and small as a local family foundation.

The people and circumstances she experienced along the way have fed her imagination and desire to write books about human relationships, her love of cooking and entertaining, and her relentless ability to find the humor in life. She writes with the sarcasm and amusement that a life fully lived provides.

She is a mother, an executive, a woman who believes that love is always present, even when it's hard to feel it. When that happens, you simply are not looking in the right places.

CPSIA information can be obtained
at www.ICGtesting.com
Printed in the USA
BVHW081139130921
616662BV00002B/108

9 781649 525925